Beneath the Pennsylvania Hills

Dedicated to Mom, Dad, Dylan, and Lucas

My angel goes with me wherever I go.
When she's not with me, I feel her eyes and I know,
Watching me through thickets, bent fields, and star-stippled air,
Wherever you are, Cecilia, I will find you there.
Pennsylvania where we met. Pennsylvania where we die. Pennsylvania where our bodies are swallowed; buried with our love and our pride.
But goodbyes are not ours for keeping, only greetings,
Until we meet again,
Somewhere in the clouds of Pennsylvania's endless empyrean.
Cecilia... Cecilia... Oh, my sweet, Cecilia...
You are my love, my road, and my eternal home.
You are my song of Pennsylvania—
Forever part of my soul...

CHAPTER 1
(1859)

It rained every day that spring. Fog cloaked the hills. Seeds floated to the top of the soil. That season, nothing grew but mud.

The Masons' land was on the ridge, considered the worst in Gold. Once again, others expected it would provide nothing that year.

The God-fearing people in the farming town of Gold blamed their father, James Mason, calling him a curse incarnate. The licentious lumberman had a reputation and was prone to endless sorts of debauchery and recidivism. The innkeepers despised him because he went from place to place without paying for his night's stay or jugs of whiskey. Prostitutes for miles resented him, regarding him as a worthless brute and miser, having suffered at the mercy of his foul tongue and irascible hand. The Mason children were practically orphaned, left alone to tend to the farm, protect themselves, and go to church without any parents to hold them in their arms, sing alongside them, or keep them warm at night, guarding their growing bodies and dreams.

At church, their small ears strained to hear the words of the Reverend Levitt Eastman each week as they sat in the back, watching him pontificate from behind his gilded pulpit.

Everything revolved around the church. Every family from Gold came together for services. It was the only place to worship for twenty miles. Beneath the whitewashed walls of the Reverend Eastman's steeple, the rich had their pews, and so did the poor.

That Sunday morning, mist fell against the Masons' thatched roof. Cecilia Mason struggled to open her eyes as she lay in bed. Her limbs weary with the weight of yesterday's work and the many days before it. Beside her, her supine elder sister Ruby, the copper crown of her head barely visible beneath the wool blanket they shared.

Each day, the thirteen-year-old rose before dawn to begin her chores. She climbed the old rickety ladder leading down from the loft, the wooden planks creaking and moaning beneath her feet.

The first thing she saw downstairs was her brother, Caleb, curled up in the corner beside the hearth, breathing in soft syncopation as he slept. The six-year-old had not uttered a word in months—not since their mother's death.

Before stepping outside, she put on a pair of oversized boots left behind by her father. The holes were large enough to fit her toes through, but the dog-eared leather was better than nothing at all.

Standing on her tip-toes, Cecilia pushed back the wooden latch to release the barn door. She removed two buckets for fetching water that hung from nails on the wall. The fading blue light of the moon was all that guided her down the familiar footpath leading behind the house and through the fields to the forest.

By the time she returned to the house, the moon was no longer visible. The emptiness of night had absolved, leaving in its wake an amalgamation of red, yellow, and orange hues—*the birth of a new day.*

"Cecilia Mason, your hair is a mess!" Ruby took hold of her, scolding her as soon as she entered the door. She shoved her down onto one of the chairs downstairs by the table. "We will be late!" Cecilia moved forward to get more comfortable. "Stay still!" Ruby yanked her back down.

"I've gotta wash up!" she squirmed.

"You should have thought of that before you dawdled and made us late!"

"I didn't *dawdle*!"

After she put Cecilia's long hair into two braids, the children followed the oxbow roads leading throughout the hills of Gold. By the time they reached the town, Caleb had dirt on his pant leg. They stopped for a few moments so Ruby could wipe it away with some spit and the hem of her skirts. Everything had to be perfect on Sundays.

Entering the church was like entering another world.

CHAPTER 2

When they arrived, the Reverend was beginning to close the doors.

"Reverend…" Ruby knelt apologetically. "I do hope that we are not late."

The Reverend stared at Ruby with his cold, steel-colored, serpent-like eyes.

"Take your places, children," his deep voice commanded. "Services will begin shortly."

He took a final look outside before closing the double-doors. Echoes stirred from the soles of his shoes as he walked with precise strides to the erect wooden plinth.

"Good morning, ladies and gentlemen," he greeted the townspeople sitting before him. His narrow shoulders lifted back so that his slender frame stood tall.

"Good morning, Reverend," they replied in unison.

"Please open your books…" He turned the pages of his own large Bible and began to read.

As he spoke, Cecilia felt his eyes on her. She could never tell whether his countenance was one of disgust or discerning wonderment for them having come at all.

"In other matters, friends," he later announced. "Mrs. Ruth Thompson passed on this week. We should all pray for her and keep the Thompson family in our hearts. Now, let us open our Hymnals…"

After services, the Reverend shook hands with members of the town, including Judge Carlson; Ms. Anna Hakes, the schoolmarm; and Mr. and Mrs. Miller, who owned a large farm as well as the local General Store.

For the children, sitting in the back did have its benefits. They were typically the first to leave, with no one paying them any mind as they walked back home together, trudging the same way they came.

"Ruby?" Cecilia asked. "Do you ever get the feeling that the Reverend doesn't like us? Like, when he's talking about bad people and sinners, and people worth spittin' on, it's like he's lookin' *right at us*. And when I look back at him, I get this bad feeling in my gut…" She pressed her hand into the pit of her stomach.

"What a dreadful thing to say!"

"I can't help it! Now you made me sorry that I told you…"

"Listen," Ruby wrapped her arm around her sister, drawing her into her side. "There's no fault in being honest, Sissy. But, sometimes, other people aren't so interested in hearing the truth you're telling."

The children arrived home and ate supper before sundown. They expected their father to appear sometime during the night. However, when Ruby, Cecilia, and Caleb awoke the next morning, they found they were still the only ones inhabiting the tiny, ill-structured shack situated within the soft, sinking crevices of the surrounding hills.

CHAPTER 3

Johnathan Wolfe rode into town bareback on his bay mare. Walking alongside him, his little black and white sheepdog, Bitsy, with her one brown eye and the other blue. Her head held high, following at the horse's feet with obsequious pride.

The first thing he noticed was a stout, balding messenger nailing a notice to a pole used for tying up horses. The man focused on the task at hand, causing his beady eyes to shrink to an even smaller size.

"Excuse me, sir?" The man continued striking his hammer. "May I ask what you are doing there?"

"Company of men is coming in to buy land!" He said with a curt smirk. "See for yourself!" He gave the nail one last hit before moving onto the next one.

John began to read:
To all landowners and proprietors in Gold,
We Want Your Land!
A.A. Vanguard and sons are willing to pay!
Make more than five-years' wages in one day!

John went to the courthouse at once.

"I'd like to see Judge Carlson, please—is he in?"

The clerk peered through the tops of his round, gold-framed glasses; his short, dark curls plastered to his head with ample amounts of pomade.

"And what is your business, Mr...?" His voice trailed.

"Name is John—Johnathan Wolfe. The Judge knows who I am, and he knows my business."

"Very well then, sir," he shut the large book he was viewing with a perturbed thud. "I shall return in a moment."

He reappeared seconds later. "He says to send you on in. This way, please, Mr. Wolfe."

He led him through a library stacked full of loose papers and legal books. When they reached a camouflaged wooden door along the back wall, the clerk knocked.

"Come in! Come in!" Clouds of tobacco smoke filled the air. "Ah, Mr. Wolfe, very good to see you. Won't you have a seat? And, uh—Kelsey?"

"Yes, sir?"

"When did these documents arrive?"

"Why..." he hesitated, struggling to recollect. "I believe it was yesterday, sir..."

"Damn it all to hell, Kelsey!" He slammed his fist on the desk. "What did I tell you? Hmm...?"

"You said to deliver them *right away*, sir."

"Right away—*right* away! And did you do that?"

"No, sir..."

"Speak up, Kelsey! Nobody likes a mumble fuss! Don't let it happen again," he began pointing emphatically with his pipe, enunciating every word with a jab, "or-next-time, it-will-be-your-job."

"Yes, sir."

"You may leave, Kelsey."

"Yes, sir."

"So, Mr. Wolfe, you're here about the Mason property, I would assume?"

"You've assumed correctly. May I see the deed please?"

"Why, yes, of course." He went to a chest of drawers, skimming through papers until he found it. "Ah! Here we are! And, may I ask, what is it you'd like with the deed, John?"

"Some men are looking to buy up the land around here. I'd like to know that everything is in order, is all."

"I see. Well, what about the matter concerns you in particular?"

"No one knows about my arrangement. Not but you and Laura Mason and her Pa, rest their souls. But now I'm looking to change over ownership."

"And, what is stopping you from telling James Mason or his children yourself about this arrangement?"

"He won't so much as let me get in his line a sight without starting to kick or swing or holler. He's never liked me much; for reasons of his own. But believe me, when I say it's best that I do not talk face to face with James Mason."

"Very well—but what about the children?"

"They have enough to sort out on their own."

"They're getting older, John. I think it's about time you sat them down and explained things to them as they stand."

"By the by—and please, forgive me for saying, Judge," he said, changing the subject. "But your clerk has an off-putting way about him."

"Yes, and might I add that you are not one of the first to say so." He removed the pipe from his mouth, bending his lips to the side in a wry smile. "Kelsey Vincent, a local sycophant," he leaned in closer. "The son of Samuel Vincent, the shoemaker, you see—but a ruffian just the same."

"Yes, I suppose that's all young men of his age."

"I'll tell you what: I'll send ol' Kelsey boy out to the Masons' to deliver the unfortunate news to Mr. James Mason in person."

"I don't reckon that's much better."

"Oh, don't you worry about Kelsey. He always seems to get the better end of the stick. But I'll tell you what: I'll send up the constable, too. Just in case there is a bit of a scuttle. What do you say?"

"I suppose now is as good a time as any to have it done and over with; state my peace."

"Good fellow, you are! I'll have it arranged right away." He let out several rings of smoke. "I can have a copy made and sent to you this Friday. Less than one week—I can't do any better than that."

"I won't ask you to."

"Very good—very good." They shook on it. "Now, heed my advice and stay away from these hapless vagabonds searching for an easy profit, John. I suspect they will find the people here in Gold aren't as impressionable as they'd like to believe. Folks here aren't so likely to part with their hard-won piece of earth. You mark my words: the people of Gold aren't going anywhere!"

CHAPTER 4

The Masons' front door flew open with Cecilia holding a rifle behind it.

"What do you want?" She aimed it at the stranger's chest–his hand suspended mid-knock. "What's your name? And what's your purpose for coming here?" She cocked back the heavy black hammer.

"Hello, young lady." He removed his gray top hat to reveal rich honey-blonde hair. It fell like silk around his clean-shaven face.

Two men on black horses waited behind him at the entrance of the Masons' wooden gate. The pair of steeds tossed their feet, meandering back and forth, clanging their metal restraints.

"The name is Alexander Vanguard," He bowed. "*Alex* for short. Is there anyone else here with you?"

"Do you think I would give an honest answer to a question like that?"

"My dear," he guffawed, "there is no need for such hostility, nor for you to hold *that* between us." He pressed his palm into the barrel of the gun. Cecilia pushed back.

She was outraged. "What? Are you wanting to get yourself killed?"

He stepped forward, trying to peer around her into the house. Ruby and Caleb hid behind the door from view. "I dare say, child, I *did* ask you a question." He swooped toward her like a hawk coming down on a field mouse. "And I do not like repeating myself." His green eyes glowered.

"Come any closer and I'll blow your head off." She felt the familiar bent steel of the trigger beneath her finger.

"Here," he scrambled to find a simple white calling card, before extending it between his index and pointer finger like a feebly foraged flag of peace. "Take this. All we want to do is offer your father or whoever is entitled to this land a decent price."

"What? This?" She motioned with her hands, questioning whether it was that exact land where they stood or if he was mistaken.

"*Yes*. Can I trust you will let whom it may concern know that I was here?"

"*No.*"

"Excuse me?"

"I won't do any such thing. I don't know you and I certainly don't *owe* you!"

She slammed the door in his face. Alex Vanguard stood in shock.

CHAPTER 5

The Masons received another visitor shortly after Alexander Vanguard had come calling.

Kelsey Vincent stood at the front door, soaking wet from the incessant rain. His auburn curls lay straight, the pomade washing down his face.

"What do you want, Kelsey?" Cecilia held her gun at her side. "You look like the groom of misery himself."

"I've brought a constable with me, Sissy. We don't want any trouble. What do you say, constable?"

"She's not used it yet, Kelsey…" he chortled. "Just keep your nerves about you, eh?"

"Thank you for your assistance," he answered dryly. "Nevertheless, this is for you."

"What is it?"

"I am performing a courtesy call to notify you of some changes which will take place in the coming days and months proximate to this property. Here are some documents, where you will find it all explained. A copy of the current deed to the house and any pertinent boundary lines is also included therein."

He quit reading from a scroll of paper and looked back at Cecilia. "It's all here." He handed her a large tube with another piece of large paper parchment rolled up in it.

"What?" Ceclia paused, taken aback. "What are you saying, Kelsey? What is it you're getting at with all this here?"

"Well, Ms. Mason. It may surprise you to know that change is expected to be coming pretty soon around here. Nothing is yet promised or certain, but they say a large number of men will be swarming to these hills here to start working. It would serve you best to review the property lines. It's easy for these wealthy men to come in and take advantage of people like you."

"Working on what?" She persisted, ignoring his insult. "Lumber camps have all moved on for now. Gold doesn't have anything anyone else could want. Just look around."

"That is where you might just be wrong, Sissy. And, if that will be all, I bid you good day. Tell Ruby I send my regards. Good evening to you." He tipped his hat and returned to his horse, leaving Cecilia feeling even more confused and unnerved.

CHAPTER 6

The carriage wheels lifted coarse clumps of mud with every labored turn. Heaps fell with soggy plunks as the burnished black stagecoach continued its ascent uphill, bouncing back-and-forth as it struggled within the road's deep ruts. Elliott Eastman pulled the collar of his wool coat tighter around his neck.

Despite the sun shining over the hills in a pellucid blue sky, the air possessed a biting chill. The 16-year-old boy and his father had been traveling for some time. They left New York City by steamship several days ago and had traveled the remaining distance by train across the rural tree-coated wilderness of Pennsylvania.

Endless hours of confinement had set in, causing an insufferable burning sensation in his legs. The overcrowded steamship had the smell of perspiration and damp air, and the unending ride in the train had jerked him uncomfortably from side to side for days.

As a distraction, he'd kept his focus on the passing scenery. Everything in the countryside was new to Elliott. For, while his father had made the trip many times before for business—up until that moment—Elliott had never left the city.

"We ain't none too far now!" Sterling, the driver, yelled as he sat on the front bench steering the team of horses through the ground's muddy mush.

"What do you think, young man?" Charles asked, closing one of his many books filled with hachured maps and notes flooding the margins.

"About what, sir?"

Charles looked out of the small carriage window as the chameleonic umbrage of green and burnt-umber forest passed like a lateral thaumatrope.

"About your new home?"

Elliott had nothing formative to say. His mind was empty. It was that way for days.

There weren't many people there. But everyone they did pass stared, gawking at the unknown faces sitting in the back of the Reverend Levitt Eastman's raven-colored stagecoach.

"It looks very different from home," he finally added feebly, staring forward. "There are no shops or buildings and fewer people and other coaches."

"Well, lucky for you, boy, your uncle has built himself the largest house in all the hills of Gold. He calls it his *Second Garden of Eden*." His father began placing his papers in an open valise. "I suspect we shall find it accommodating, to say the least. My brother was never one for living meagerly. But, *this* is home now."

"Will I be going to school?" He had not been in a schoolroom for more than a year. He'd stopped attending last winter when his mother had fallen ill.

"I am sure your uncle will have everything sorted. He is a well-established man here. You will see. He will provide you with everything you need. Education and otherwise."

Now that his mother was gone, Elliott felt utterly alone in the world. Perhaps his uncle and Gold would help to change that, he thought.

Night and day his father kept to himself, locked in his basement laboratory busying himself with work; often leaving their tenement in New York for weeks to meet others, visiting those interested in his scientific discoveries and experiments in other places throughout the country. The boy worried his father would one day leave and abandon him completely, shattering any hope of a bond between them, any inkling of an iota of care.

When they arrived at the front of his uncle Levitt's house, Sterling unfettered their belongings from the back and sides of the carriage.

"Gentlemen," he said. "Please follow me."

Elliott looked around at the sprawling expanse of manicured grounds. Espaliering ivy flowed over the brick and mortar stone of the massive 'L'-shaped edifice.

"I fear I should get lost in a place like this," Elliott looked around in awe.

"Just mind your uncle Levitt," his father told him, "and all will be fine."

A woman dressed in a plain gray and white maid's uniform greeted them at the front door. "Good afternoon Mr. Eastman—young master Eastman," she bowed. "I am glad to see you have arrived safely. My name is Mrs. Loudermilk. Please let me know if I can be of assistance to you. I must inform you, with regret, that your uncle was called away to a meeting of the local parishioners a short while ago. He has asked me to show you to your rooms and around the grounds, and ensure you have everything you need for the time being."

"Thank you very much, Mrs. Loudermilk. We do appreciate you being here to greet us—Has my brother gone very far?"

"No, no, dear. Only a few towns over. He will be returning tomorrow evening."

"Oh, I see. In that case, please take me straight to my room. I wish to get my things in order."

"Why of course, sir. Right, this way."

Mrs. Loudermilk led them through several corridors decorated with petrified animals. Pain, fear, and defiance cemented in their lacquered gaze. Forever frozen in death.

"Your uncle likes to hunt." Mrs. Loudermilk said, as though she had heard his thoughts. "It takes him away quite often." Elliott found their tortured and twisted faces profoundly haunting, and wondered how one could derive a sense of joy from such pain?

"Here are your rooms, Mr. Eastman. You will find fresh linens on the bed and extras in the cupboard. There is also water in the basin beside the washtub, changed three times daily. Towels are on the stand," she pointed. "Please notify me of anything else that you may need or that you require at this time. There will be someone making rounds within these halls regularly, and I will be nearby at all times. My room is down the hall, before you get to the other servant's quarters."

His father's doors closed and he was left alone with Mrs. Loudermilk.

"Mrs. Loudermilk?" They started back through the corridor.

"Yes, dear? Oh, and you may call me Esther if you would prefer."

"Thank you—My aunt Emily—is she here?"

"She is, dear. But, I must confess, she isn't quite in a place to receive visitors. You are aware of her, oh my..." she hesitated. "How do I say this? Well, her *condition?*"

Elliott had never met his aunt. He knew that she had suffered from a series of disabling strokes several years ago. However, other than that, much of her condition and other areas of her life had remained unknown to him. His mother would talk of her from time to time. However, his father refused to mention a word.

"Yes ma'am. I was wondering if I might be able to see her?"

Elliott could tell the question had made the amicable woman uncomfortable. Her small, nervous eyes darted from side-to-side, searching for someone who might overhear. "I'm afraid...," she hesitated for a moment. "Well, I'm afraid your uncle doesn't care much for her receiving visitors."

"I am aware she suffered a stroke some time back, and I have been told that she can no longer speak with others. I suppose, well, being her family and all, Mrs. Loudermilk, would I not be permitted to see her? I can wait until another time, any time that is appropriate. I assure you I mean to be no bother."

"Oh, it's no bother, dear. I shall see what I can do and will let you know. But, it likely won't happen today."

"Yes, ma'am. I understand."

"She is in a private wing. But, you see, what I think is best is if you were to ask your uncle Levitt yourself when he arrives back at the manor."

"Yes, ma'am?"

"Yes, dear. He may be interested in hearing your exact intentions and I think those are best relayed by you."

"Yes, Mrs. Loudermilk."

They proceeded through the long halls with red carpets until they reached another set of dark, wood-colored, double-doors, similar to his father's rooms.

"Here are your rooms, Elliott." She fumbled with her collection of keys gathered on a heavy brass ring. "Is there anything else I can get for you, my dear?" She walked in and pinned back the drapes, then bent over the bed to prop up the pillows and straighten the sheets.

She walked busily around the bed, inspecting each corner to make sure that every inch was tucked in. "If that is all then, I will leave you to get settled in. I do very much imagine that you are tired after so much traveling."

"Yes, ma'am."

Elliott looked around, his breath increasing with the unwelcome sensation of utter trepidation. He felt a pang of loneliness reverberate throughout him. He did not want the older woman to leave, even though she was a practical stranger.

"You seem like a very nice young man, Elliott. I truly look forward to having you here." She gave him a friendly smile again. "Get some rest. And don't hesitate to come find me anytime you need anything."

"Thank you, Mrs. Loudermilk."

"Any time, dear." The doors closed, and Elliott was left alone with the prospect of sleep and the sepulchral silence of his new home.

CHAPTER 7

That evening, James Mason ate with ravenous delight beside the flickering light of the hearth's fire. The shadows dancing from the flames exaggerated every line indenting his weathered face. His short, dark hair clung to the beads of sweat collecting against the base of his neck.

"This'n's good." He said, shoveling food into his mouth.

"Would you like some more, Papa?" Ruby asked.

"No, no." He grabbed his bulging midsection. "My belly is right full n' up there."

"Papa…" Cecilia began, "Before you leave again, there's something you should see."

"What is it?" he grumbled.

"Kelsey Vincent brought something up the other day…"

"Seeking my arrest I suspect—well I don't give no damn!"

"Here," Cecilia handed him the document. "See for yourself."

"What are you doing?" He raised his hand as if to hit her, causing her to instinctively shrink away. "You know I can't make out a word of this gibbergaff, you little ingrate! Ruby!" He bellowed. "What does it say?"

Of all the Mason children, she was the only one who could read, learning from the schoolmarm, Ms. Anna Hakes, whom she did laundry for once every week.

"Here," he shoved it into Ruby's face.

"Well—um," her voice quivered, knowing the one who delivered the news was likely to see the worst of his blows. "Well, you see, it says we need to review the deed…"

"Out with it!" He threw his hands on the table and leaned forward. "Stop your stutterin' and outright tell me what that damned thing says!"

"It says it belongs to someone else!" Cecilia blurted. "The house our land sits on belongs to John Wolfe. Mama's daddy gave it over to him when he died, not you. And—"

"You're a dirty liar!" He cut her off. "That supposed to be funny, you little piece a horse tar? You think because I can't read, I'll be made a fool of?"

He tore up the parchment. "I'll show you," he grumbled. "This house belongs to me, and it *always* will. How dare someone try n' take what's rightfully mine?"

"It belonged to grandad, and he had every right to give it over to John," said Cecilia.

"You!" He pointed at her, eyes brimming with fury. "You ain't never been on my side! Just like your mother; you stick up for him. For that, John!" Throwing his chair behind him, he broke it against the wall.

The children scattered. Ruby grabbed Caleb and ran for the door. Furniture scraped around as James struggled to catch Cecilia. He stared her down, both standing on opposite sides of the kitchen table, his eyes full of ire, hands bracing the wood grain of the table so hard it groaned. Grinning like a cat that had trapped its prey in the corner, he lurched forward, causing her to jump.

"I'll catch you and squeeze you till' the blood pools outcher' eyes and ears, ya little snake!"

Cecilia took a deep breath and dashed for the back door, ripping it open so hard she thought it might fall from the frame.

She flew through the dark. Not stopping to catch her breath, and not to look back. She kept her eyes on the black outline of the forest until it swallowed her.

"I'll rattle you, girl!" He yelled, his voice echoing throughout the hills. "Show yourself and get back here or I'll kill ya, I will!"

Once she reached the clearing, she crouched down behind a large oak tree along the water, remaining still. She could hear her father pounding through the branches behind her, becoming short of breath.

"You can't hide forever, girl! Remember that! I'll be back! I'll be back for ya! I'm gonna hack you into critter fodder with my ax—you'll pay, you will!" He spit, kicking the ground. "You'll see, you little ungrateful child of a whore, I'll make you pay!" She tucked her head into her knees, muffling her breath until she was certain he had left.

In the morning, after falling asleep intermittently throughout the cold, miserable night, she was jolted awake by the cautious touch of a man's hand. She gasped. Thinking it was her father. But, when her eyes fell into focus, she realized it was John.

"Morning, Sissy." He removed his hat. "Didn't mean to startle you. I take it you had a night did you?"

"I didn't sleep as well as I usually do, if that's what you mean," she said, picking a leaf out of her hair.

"I spoke with the Judge, Sissy. I knew he was sending Kelsey up to deliver the news. I was hoping to beat your Pa home but it looks like I didn't. Caught up with Ruby and Caleb not too far down the road and they told me what happened. I took them up to my place and came back to look for you. You alright?"

"Yes," she nodded. "Just tired and a little hungry."

"Alright then," he took her hand, pulling her up. "Let's get you back with your brother and sister. You can stay with me for as long as you would all like."

"I can't ask you for something like that, John."

"You didn't ask me anything, Sissy," he said, helping her onto the back of his horse.

As they rode, she fought back the urge to sleep. They followed the creek back to his cabin, Bitsy trotting alongside.

"I appreciate everything you've done for me—well, all of us—you've been such a help, especially since Mama died."

"Your ma and I were close." His hands clutched the reins. "We were raised like brother and sister."

"Why do you think she married a man like my pa, John? What could she have seen in him? Sometimes I think there isn't any part of him there to love. He's just an ignorant brute better off wandering this world alone."

"You should know he was different back then. He fought harder than anybody to get your mama. He wasn't always so mean. People do change. Some for the better, and some for the worse."

"Would you tell me how you came to know them again? How you came to live with Mama and Granddaddy?"

"You already know how all that came to be."

"I'd like to hear it again. It's a nice story."

"Is that so?"

"You know it is," she smiled. "Anyway, how did Mama find you?"

"She fell right through the snow on a perfectly white winter day. Through a bunch of leaves and branches I had put over top of a house cellar. The house had burned down, I figured. Everything was covered in ash. I had been sleeping there beneath the ground with a chicken on each side to keep warm. She came crashing through and sent them scattering, feathers and all. She began to cry, because her leg broke. She wasn't scared to see me there, not as scared as I was to see her. But, she had those deep, pleading eyes asking me for help. So, I carried her back to your Grandaddy's house and we got on. He offered me a meal and later, a place to stay. I didn't have any family and they treated me well enough like their own. And there's your story, Sissy."

They arrived at John's cabin in the Black Woods after close to an hour of riding at a slow, easy pace. It was always dark where he lived, shrouded by a dense patch of pine trees.

The children were happy to see each other, and Cecilia was grateful for a warm place next to the caste iron stove. John cooked breakfast for them. The smell of sizzling bacon and frying eggs inundated the cozy cabin. They stared at the browning meat John stirred when a 'thud' against the wall broke their attention.

"What was that?" Cecilia asked.

"Everyone get down! Cover your heads!" John moved a bearskin rug revealing a metal ring on the floor. Opening it, he placed the children in the crawl space concealed beneath the floorboards. He motioned for them once more to be quiet before closing it, leaving them to wait in the dark.

They could hear John moving across the floor. Taking a piece of white linen hanging from a nail on the wall, he tore it into one long piece and tied it to the end of a stick before hanging it out the window. The thudding stopped. It had been arrows. John stuck his head up and looked out at the assailants.

"*I surrender,*" he called out in his native language.

"*Discard your weapons and show your face,*" their leader replied. He appeared to be elderly but was firm with his words.

"Nya:wëh, travelers." John said, meaning hello. "The name is John Wolfe and this is my home."

"My name is Blacksnake and I am the leader of this tribe. Reveal yourself!"

John opened the door, hands open, palms facing upward to show that he had nothing to hide.

"You are not what we expected to see," the leader rode toward him on his dapple-gray appaloosa.

"You were expecting someone who isn't Native?"

"Yes."

"And why is that?"

"We have been pushed further south from fur trappers moving in from the north in New York. They used to stay in their own towns but now, they are claiming everywhere. There is no limit to what they will take. We thought you might be one of them—one of them that burned our land."

"They did the same thing to my people—years back now," John told them. "That is how I came to live here, in Gold. Tell me, what is it that you seek here?"

"What we seek is what you would believe: shelter and sustenance. But there is something else..." He motioned with his hands. *"Bring it forward. Hurry now! We need a safe place to keep the few precious belongings we have left. We followed the path of the highest hills."*

Eight young men appeared behind the leader, revealing half-a-dozen chests filled with several pure gold bars and other valuables. They set them down with a heavy clunk.

"*Do you know of a place which is safe to hide these things?*"

"*I do. And I will tell you. It is protected by rattlesnakes. They cover the entire floor of a hidden cave. So even if one were to find the cave, it isn't likely they will make it through to take it with them.*" John raised his finger in the air, pointing. "*You follow this road here. It continues through the pines for a mile; then, you will reach the fields—look to the highest point. Go there. You will find the cave hidden beneath some pines on the north side of the tallest hill.*"

"*I see. Thank you, John. We will be leaving now, but perhaps we will cross paths once again one day. Before we go, please take these gold pieces as a sincere thank you for your help today.*"

The leader and the others departed. But before they did, John gave them some food to take with them. He then returned to the house. Upon hearing footsteps, the children did not know whether to be paralyzed with terror or relieved. When the floor hatch was thrown open, they were put at ease to see it was John.

"Who were they?" Cecilia immediately asked.

"They are from another clan close to mine. It was taken over by some people and they're looking for shelter."

"Do you know them?"

"In a way, *yes*."

He put his hat back on his head, the brown canvas dented and worn from years of handling.

"John?"

"Yes, Sissy?"

"Will you take us home?"

"*This minute?* But what about your pa?"

"I'm tired of running and I'm tired of hiding. Next time he comes home, I'll be ready for him."

"It's an easy thing to say, Sissy, but—"

"I don't need you to believe me. Either way, John, I've got to stop backing down. And that's the way it's going to be from here out. I won't be chased and hunted down no more. I'm going to be like you—I'm going to stand up and do what's right. I can't keep on this way. All this with my pa stops *here and now*."

"I want you to take something." He held out the gold pieces in his hand, placing them in Cecilia's palm. "Hide them well and wait for a time when you need to use them the most. This way, you won't ever have to sell anything to get by or waste time wanting things in life. All you should need from now on to survive, Sissy, is love."

CHAPTER 8

On Monday morning, the halls of the Eastman house possessed an eerie quiescence. Each room dressed for a visitor, despite a despondence that pervaded for years. A full set of twelve plates with accompanying silverware lined the dining room table, changed each day before they could collect a thin covering of dust. The only one privileged enough to use the fine-dining ware was the Reverend Levitt Eastman. That is, before Elliott and his father arrived.

Emily Eastman took her meals in her room. Isolated, she sat in a rocking chair. The front grounds and distant hills hazily replicated in her glassy stare. A servant would come every morning and tie back her black and silver strands of hair into a tight knot behind her ears. Other than these and a few other simple things, living for Emily Eastman had ceased long ago. The Eastman estate's only other inhabitants were the six or so servants on the grounds, scattered yet intact, like perfunctory organs.

Outside it poured. The tall walls of Elliott's room echoed with the sound of the rain. He moved from the bed to the built-in bench beside the large French windows. Across the courtyard, he saw droplets falling from the glossy leaves of ivy crawling up the parapet. Two crows picked at worms in the damp earth.

A knock on the door woke him from his semi-waking state, eyes muddled by his own thoughts. He was hoping to see either his father or his uncle, who had not yet returned.

"Yes?"

"Mr. Eastman?" A petite, young brunette stood on the other side; she looked no more than eighteen with cherubic sanguine cheekbones.

"I am here to see if you need anything, sir?"

"No, thank you."

"If that is all then." She turned to leave.

"Wait! There is something."

"Sir?"

"Please, call me, Elliott."

"Very well."

"Where can I find a riding horse?"

"Do you need a carriage into town? I can have it arranged."

"No. That's not it. To be honest with you, I never rode much in the city, or before now. I suppose because you can walk anywhere…" he stuck his hands into his pockets. "Maybe I should wait then..." He looked out the window. The sun was beginning to come out, if only for a moment.

"I see. Well, if you go to the stables, Thatcher Turner should be able to help you with what you need."

"And what is your name?"

"Maggie."

"Thank you, Ms. Maggie."

"Do you know how to get to the stable, Elliott?"

"No, but I'm sure I'll manage."

"Look," she went to the window. "Do you see that large building down there?"

"Yes…"

"That's the one. The one next to it is for the cows. That big one is where you'll find Thatcher."

"And, is Mrs. Loudermilk available today?"

"Esther?"

"Yes."

"She is. Should I send her up?"

"No. That will be alright. I should like to get to know the place a bit more. I am confident I will find her eventually."

"Very well then." She curtsied once more.

Elliott decided to venture outside, studying the rooms as he passed. He was tired of feeling caged. He went by a tall wooden door leading to Levitt's library. Next, a generous study with a roaring fireplace. Although Levitt's killed quarry was displayed throughout the house, this room contained his feats from other countries, such as two lions from the Savannah and an elephant from India. The desk his uncle had was at the opposite end of the fireplace, facing all these prisoners of his self-proclaimed war of pride.

He found a spiral staircase and went downstairs to the atrium where he could see the front of the grounds through the door's long, glass windows. He was reaching for the doorknob when Sterling stepped in front of him.

"Can I help you, young master Elliott?"

"No thank you, Sterling," he answered, knowing he would likely object if he told him his intentions. "I am stretching my legs for a moment," he lied.

"Be careful. Wouldn't want us to get lost

now, would we?"

"No, sir. Thank you."

"Better watch yourself, boy."

"What did you say?" At first, he couldn't believe his ears. "Why would I need to do that?"

"Because young men who cause trouble don't remain in the house of a holy man for long." Sterling watched him closely as he walked away.

So, instead of going out, he decided to look for Mrs. Loudermilk. The kitchen was on the first floor. It did not take him too long to find it. Mrs. Loudermilk was standing over a pot of boiling water with a wooden spoon in her hand; her neck and shoulders sloping forward from years of the same hard work.

"Mrs. Loudermilk?"

"Oh, my dear!" she let out a gasp, her hand flying to her chest. "You gave me a start!"

"I'm sorry. I—"

"Don't be sorry, dear! Come here," she pulled out a chair from the nearby table. "Come and sit for a minute. I spend plenty of time here by myself. Now, why don't you tell me some things about yourself?"

"I am afraid I have done something to make Sterling cross. He permits me no freedom nor warmth of character."

"Oh, you cannot worry about him. He's been like that for years. Always telling on another. Little bits here and there to get people roused or stirred up. Oh, and what he tells your uncle," she lowered her voice. "It's a wonder any of us are able to stay here at all. You must ignore him, Elliott. You'll get used to things soon enough, and start to know who is who and what is what. Then you'll be telling him what to do." She winked.

"What are you making?"

"Oh, where to begin?" She put her small, flour-coated hands on her hips. Luckily, she was wearing an apron. "Biscuits and potatoes for breakfast. Something sweet for later. But we'll save that for a surprise."

"How long have you worked here, Esther?"

"About," she thought about it, "going on ten years now."

"Do you see my aunt, Emily, often?"

"Oh, no, dear, I'm afraid not. After she became ill, your uncle decided to hire on additional hands to help with her condition and to take care of her at all hours of the day. She requires constant attention. In case she were to fall from bed or her chair. She wasn't always so, though. I knew her before the accident."

"But, I thought she was left permanently paralyzed? How could she fall, if that is true? How could she move about at all?"

"Oh, don't listen to what I say..." She waved the thought away. "She *is* paralyzed, dear. It's just that sometimes she gets these fits. They send her limbs and arms flailing about, I'm told."

"Does my aunt ever leave her room?"

"No," she said quickly. "Your uncle will not allow it."

"Why not?"

"You may have to ask him such a question, I suppose. But, if I were to venture, I suspect he fears it will happen again—something like what happened before."

"What exactly *did* happen to her, Esther?"

"Oh, I do think it's best if you discuss such things with your uncle, dear. It's really not my place to say. But, would you like something to drink? I've already put a kettle on for tea."

"Yes, please."

She put down two porcelain saucers and cups and poured.

"Your aunt is the one who hired me, as she did many of the people who still work here today. Your uncle was often gone, and still is, as you may have noticed. He hasn't changed much since I've been here. Mrs. Eastman is the one that many came to know. Her voice is the one that carried through the halls, beckoning me and the others here and there. Something about it, I do believe I actually enjoyed," she smiled. "But, when she fell ill, it became quiet. A very *strange* kind of quiet."

"But you do not know what caused it?"

Her face became troubled. She looked around, getting up to peer outside the double-doors.

"Okay, I'll tell you what happened. But you cannot tell another soul."

"Yes, I understand."

"It rained a lot that day, you see. The day it happened. People weren't leaving the house. Even the animals in the barn were moved to prevent them from drowning. The water rose for days. Everyone suspected it would flood. But, I never saw something like that in my life. Not like that day.

"Your uncle was here, helping with the cows

and horses. Said he had a premonition. Just kept murmuring to himself saying, *'trouble's coming. Trouble's coming to them Masons.'*

"They live just over the hill. Poor as church mice. Never had a thing to do with that family before that day. But, for some reason, here he was, rushing on off over the hill. Got it in his head he was to help them, those Masons. So, despite your aunt's begging and pleading, he took off through the forest. I remember seeing him. Something strange in his eyes.

"Your aunt waited hours for him to come home. But, after a while, she couldn't wait any longer. Others offered to go out and look for him but she said that wouldn't be right, others risking their life. She was the one who decided she'd go out and try to bring him home. The next thing we heard was your uncle hollering for help, carrying your aunt in his arms. Said she'd collapsed out there from all the excitement, and it'd caused her to fall off her horse and hit her head. Never really knew what happened outside of that. But that's what he told us."

"Do you think she could ever get better?"

"I would like to think that she can, Elliott. But, I don't like to talk about that day or think about it."

"Thank you, Esther."

"It's your family, Elliott. You should know. Besides, your aunt loved you from the minute you were born and was *so* fond of your mother as well."

Just then Sterling came through the swinging doors.

"Elliott," he said snidely. "Why are you here?" He didn't wait for an answer. "The morning meal will be served shortly. You should be in the dining room."

"Thank you, Sterling," Esther said. "You are always most helpful and it is *always* appreciated." She flashed him a cheery smile.

"Yes, well." He jolted up, straightening his hunched back. "I am most assured that the boy is in capable hands with you, Esther. Like a mother to all, aren't we? And, Elliott?" He included before she could utter an answer.

"Yes?"

"Your uncle says you're not to travel about or leave the estate without someone to accompany you. He will be returning tonight before supper."

"But what if I—"

"I'm afraid we must adhere strictly to those terms. Now, if you have any issue, I think it best to take it up with your uncle when he returns."

"Yes, sir."

"See you promptly in 30 minutes in the dining hall," he said, looking with a sharp, surreptitious stare as he used his back to exit the scullery doors.

"Stiff, he is," she said, speaking to Elliott. "But he does have a way of hiding himself about this place." She leaned closer to Elliott. "Just be careful what you do and say around him," she whispered. "He's your uncle's eyes and ears, that one."

CHAPTER 9

Cecilia walked through the knee-high amber grass. The tasseled edges slapped against her open palm as she passed, bent and broken from the weight of gathering raindrops. She trudged through the sodden fields to the forest behind the house. It stopped raining, and the sun appeared for the first time in days.

She went to the clearing beside the creek. Bending over to remove her boots, she took off her clothing except for the plain white shift she wore underneath. Despite the brisk air, she wanted to get into the water. Working all day tilling the fields made her sweat. No matter how cold it was most of the time.

She walked through the water until it became deep enough to swim. There were some areas near the center where it was possible. It became shallow once more just before a small isolated patch of land, a weeping willow at its center.

Cecilia went to the tree and curled up at the base of it, feeling the familiar edges of its bark against her skin. She laid her head back and rested her eyes. The tree seemed to create an enveloping warmth, like a loving family member welcoming her home.

The last thing she remembered before she fell asleep was the lulling whistle of the wind and a few scattered birds in the trees chattering amongst themselves. Only a few moments had passed when the sound of a snapping tree branch startled her awake.

"Who's there?" She called across the creek. "I know you're there! Show yourself!"

Slowly, Elliott Eastman appeared from behind the base of an oak tree large enough to conceal him.

"I'm very sorry, miss. I did not mean to give you a fright."

"Give me a fright?" She laughed at the absurdity. "*You're* the one who should be frightened. Don't you know you're trespassing?"

"Sorry, miss?"

"This land doesn't belong to you and you don't belong *on it*. Who are you anyway?"

"My name is Elliott." He removed his cap, grasping it with both hands. "Elliott Eastman."

"Are you any relation to the Reverend Eastman?"

"Yes. That is my uncle."

"My name is Cecilia, but most call me, Sissy—Sissy Mason."

"Sissy," he repeated. "It is nice to meet you. If you kindly point me in the right direction, I'll be on my way."

"Just give me a moment to get my clothes." After putting on her clothes, she came to stand by this seemingly innocuous, but by all accounts handsome, stranger. "How in the world did you ever end up here? I've never seen you before. Not in church or town…"

"We've come to live with my uncle. I've been inside for days because of the rain. So, since there was a break, I decided I'd venture out. I suppose I wandered too far and lost my way."

"The Reverend's house isn't too far away. Don't worry. You are lost but you haven't gone too far. It's just over the hill about three miles."

"That is a bit of a distance by foot."

"Well, please don't take offense, but your uncle is wealthy. Why don't you take one of his horses to ride?

"I tried. This man made it so I felt I had to flee."

"Flee your own home?" She gave him a look, indicating she thought the idea outrageous. "That could only be that greasy crow of a side shackle he hides up there in that manor of his–that *Sterling*."

Elliott laughed. "That's incredible! You are absolutely right. It *was* him."

"He's unforgivably joined to your uncle, like a door to its hinge." Cecilia inhaled deeply and looked down at her modest clothing. It was dry. But it was sheer and hung loosely from her arms like a lampshade. She placed her arms over her stomach and chest, suddenly uncomfortable.

"Are you cold? Do you need something?"

"No. I'll be just fine. But you better get moving if you'd like to make it back before it starts raining again, or worse yet, gets dark."

She led him back through the woods toward Levitt's. They walked on, both silent for several moments until Elliott, who could bear it no longer, decided to speak.

"Do you live close to here?"

"I do. Just on the other side of the creek."

"Do you go there often?"

"Oh, yes. It's one of my favorite places. I can be alone, and it's quiet."

"You like it? Being alone?"

"Sometimes, yes. Why? You don't?"

"Not particularly. I'm alone too often."

"I suppose that's the thing about most people."

"What's that?"

"Always wanting something other than what they have." She changed the subject. "Do you have any brothers or sisters?"

"No," he shook his head.

"You're lucky."

"Why is that?"

"I spend all day with my brother and sister. They're not the most agreeable company–always following me or needing something." She smiled at Elliott. "You will have to believe me at my word."

"That I do."

They walked uphill until the grassy path curved through a shaded ridge covered on both sides by hemlocks and pines. The air became colder and dark. They continued until reaching a set of open fields, where the gabled roof of Levitt's manor became visible in the distance.

"Your uncle's house is just over there. Do you see it?"

"Yes!" he exclaimed. "Please," he began, filled with gratitude, "could I extend an invitation for you to sit with us at dinner?"

"Oh, no!" She replied, looking abashedly down at her dirty bare feet. "That's quite alright."

"I would like to do something to thank you, Sissy."

"There's no need, Elliott. Any decent person would have done it. Perhaps I'll see you in town one of these days. Most likely at church, I'd imagine."

"I certainly will look for you. I mean, I expect I will go with my uncle. If it's the same church."

"There's only one church in Gold," she answered, smiling. "See you Sunday."

CHAPTER 10

"Sissy! Where have you been? You were supposed to be home hours ago! Where are the buckets?"

"I forgot. I'll go back."

"Oh no you don't." Ruby grabbed her sister by the shirt collar and pulled her to the table. "Sit down."

"What about dinner?"

"I've taken care of it. When you didn't come back, I went down to the creek looking for you myself, but you weren't there. That's when I found these." She bent down, picking up the two tin buckets Cecilia had left behind. "Don't lose these, Sissy! We can't afford to replace them."

"Yes, Ruby."

"Now wash your face and get ready for supper."

As Cecilia prepared to clean her hands in the gray water of the wash basin, something tipped over a metal can outside. Then she heard her father's deep churlish voice curse.

"Is that Papa?"

"Yes," she frowned. "He came home just a little bit ago. Took a bath and said he's expecting Lyman Steele any minute."

"Lyman Steele?" she repeated in disbelief. "What's he doing coming around here?"

"I don't know," she whispered. "He didn't explain. Just came in here barking orders and then demanded water for his bath. Thank goodness you're back though," she added.

"Nobody comes for Papa unless he owes them."

"Sissy, I told you, I can't say why. Just do as you're told and don't cause no trouble tonight. Hopefully it's all over and done with soon enough."

She went upstairs to the loft and began fixing her hair with the flat of her palm, praying it would lay down flat. Luckily, her swim in the creek had washed away any smudges of dirt on her face, arms, and legs. She grabbed one of Ruby's dresses and threw it on, hoping her sister would not notice.

"Hey! That's mine!" Ruby called as soon as she spotted Cecilia coming down the loft's ladder.

"Mine's dirty, Ruby. I'll have to borrow it…"

"Have to *nothing,* Sissy Mason," she hissed. "I told you to stop running around like something wild and knotting up your hair and bruising and scraping your knees to bits!"

"Well, now, what is this?" James Mason came into the room, fully shaved and dressed in his best. "Why—are my wee darling little angels fighting?"

"No, sir." Ruby went back to stirring the pot of broth she had stewing upon the stove. "We was just discussing the state of Sissy's clothes, is all—she's got none."

He threw his hand up under his chin in a fist.

Ruby flinched, gasping. "Don't sass me, ungrateful, no-for-good… Keep settin' the table!" She put a bowl in front of them all, including an extra one for their guest.

"What is this? Is this all we're having?" James threw out a spoonful of stew, watching with disgust as it sloshed back into the bowl. He stomped his foot, lunging toward Ruby who nearly fell back.

"It's all we could afford, Papa. We're running out of money, and food, and we don't have too many things left to make due with…" she explained.

"*Make due…*" he spat. "This isn't good enough for swine lyin' in the mud let alone my company! Now, get this out of here! We need some meat! A real meal! Not this horse tar trash!" He took the porcelain dish in his hand and hurled it against the wooden wall. The steaming liquid streaked down like rain on a dusty window. "I expect something on the table by the time I come back in. Otherwise, I'll be sending one of you *away without no remorse*." It was one of his favorite phrases. "That should make it a little easier to *make due*!" He went outside, slamming the door.

"Sissy," Ruby approached her in a panic. "What are we going to do?"

"I don't know what we *can* do, Ruby. He's unreasonable as sin. We just don't have any meat to give him."

"Then what are we supposed to feed him and Lyman Steele?"

Cecilia called for Caleb, taking a rag and dipping it into a bucket of water they kept beside the hearth in the kitchen. "Take the soap and start cleaning up the soup Papa just spilled, okay? Good boy." She turned back to Ruby. "We've got no chickens. The cow we need for milking. The only possible thing we could spare is Elsie."

"We can't kill the horse! Are you crazy?"

"What else are we supposed to do, Ruby?"

"There has to be another way… Lyman handles dead animals all the time. You don't think he'll notice?"

"Well, if there is another way," she said, looking out the window at their father as he stood with his back to them. Smoke rolled. Tobacco oscillating into the cool evening air. "You better think of it fast, because I've already said what's come to my mind."

"Damn!" Ruby cried in frustration. She rarely swore. "Fine. Just make it fast." She hung her head in defeat. "I don't want to have time to think about it."

Cecilia took off with her rifle to the small, sideways barn behind the house. Elsie stood tied to a post. Her ears perked back as the door yanked open. She looked back at Cecilia, her eyes sad and knowing.

"Hey there, girl." She went over to the elderly mare, stroking her back as she spoke soft words to her. "I'm sorry, Elsie. I don't want to have to do this—please don't remember me for this, girl."

She picked up the gun, which she had propped nearby against the wall. Standing back, she aimed at the back of the horse's matted head, closed her eyes, and fired.

As the hacked-off slabs burned in the pan, Cecilia and Ruby fought back the urge to cry.

"Ruby!" She tried to remain calm and keep her voice down but found it difficult. "Ruby! I think he's here."

"Well, quick! Get these onto the plates. It's a little rare yet but it will have to do."

"What do you suppose we should say it is?"

"I don't know. Just, don't say anything if no one asks."

"But what if he does?"

"They're not gonna. Now just go!"

Caleb and Cecilia sat at the table while Ruby served the food, her hands nervously shaking.

"Children!" The door came crashing open. "Pull up a seat for our guest!"

"Hello, Mr. Steele. How do you do?" Ruby attempted to disguise her disgust from the stench and sight of him.

Lyman Steele was the town taxidermist. He lived in a large house, not too far from the schoolteacher Ms. Anna Hakes, who the Mason children often visited. He enjoyed his job of stuffing and preserving animals in a manner most found quite odd, spending hours alone in his giant, empty house, shuttered, cold, and dark. His appearance was wild. Tall and lanky, his dark hair stuck straight on end, his skin red and blotchy, and his smell utterly repellent, like dried blood and rotting flesh—Death. Worst of all were his merciless and menacing glowing green eyes.

"Ruby." He removed his hat and bowed; his shoulder-length, stringy hair greased back for the occasion. "How are you?"

"Very well, thank you."

"Cecilia," he turned to her. "These… these are for you." He pushed a crumpled bouquet of dead daisies into her face.

"Thanks," she said dryly. "I'll get water for them."

"So, Lyman," Ruby said, wiping her hands on her apron. "How are you? Please, have a seat."

"Uh-hm…," he coughed, clearing his throat. "I suppose that'n be the thing to do."

"Right," Ruby replied wryly. "Papa, would you care to say some words before we eat?"

"Phfft! You know we don't do that around here, girl. Now don't be wasting any more of a man's precious time," he winked at Lyman. "Hand me those rolls there."

"Here, Papa," Cecilia handed him the plate of bread and butter before he could say anymore.

"Thank you, Sissy. That's mighty nice of yuns. And that's my girl! Always there to serve a man when and what it is he needs." He took a huge bite from the meat, leaving a stringy tendon dangling from the corner of his mouth as he continued to chew and talk. "Delicious! And so tender!"

Lyman gave a slight nervous grin. Knowing animals his entire life and what they looked like on the inside, Cecilia was sure he suspected it wasn't beef. He didn't say much during the meal. Luckily, James Mason was his typical self and too pompous to care what others had to say.

"Not much of an appetite this evening there, Lyman?"

"I'm 'fraid I et' some before I came. Wasn't expecting all this much…"

"No need ta' feel sorry for it there," James said. "More for me when ya leave," he added, roaring with laughter.

"Mr. Mason?" he began when they had finished. "Could we step outside? There is something I been fixing to discuss with you."

"You got a pipe?"

"Yes, sir?"

"Well bring it on along then and let's go do some talking–just us men."

The girls sent Caleb up to their bed in the loft while they waited downstairs. Although the men were not far away, the details they discussed remained obscure, muffled by the walls.

When Lyman left, James Mason came in with an alarmingly large smile on his face.

"Well, I would say that went well, wouldn't you?" He looked at Cecilia.

"*What* went well?" Cecilia questioned skeptically.

"Ah, there you go again, Sissy." He came over to her, ruffling her hair. "Always trying to ruin the surprise Papa has in store."

"What are you doing? Stop this and tell us now!"

"You foul-tongued little wretch… I suppose there's no better time to tell you that I plan to collect a dowry from Mr. Steele."

"A dowry?" Ruby was shocked. "What for?"

"For my little girl's hand in marriage."

"What? You're marrying me off, Papa?"
"No, Ruby. Not you. Your sister, *Sissy*."
"No!" The girls cried out. Caleb came running to Cecilia, wrapping his arms around her.
"You can't do this, Papa!" Ruby screamed. The children formed a shield around each other.
"*I can.* And *I have*."

CHAPTER 11

Time passed slowly for Elliott who waited anxiously for Sunday, when he hoped to see Cecilia. Keeping busy in his uncle's library, he read Milton or Melville, or ambled about the grounds. He had even looked for his father near the stables. In the whole time they had been there, Elliott had not seen him more than half a dozen times.

Eventually, he was able to convince his uncle to allow him to take a horse into town. He had gone on a few occasions since moving to Gold, and had met a few different people; including Jacob Miller, the son of a local farmer who was also the owner of Gold's only general store.

"Hey there, Elliott! How are you today?" Jacob stood behind the counter wearing a white clerk's apron.

"What can I get for you?"

"I was looking for books. Sadly, I've read all the ones in Levitt's library."

"Well, this is what we have in at the moment," he pointed to a shelf brimming mostly with biblical texts and religious authors, a smaller mirror of his uncle's collection.

"Do you have anything else?"

"I could order something special with our next shipment of goods," he suggested. "What were you looking for?"

"Possibly some Poe… Thoreau… or Whitman?"

"Whitman? Is he new?"

"Sort of."

"Okay." He said, putting down his pen and folding the piece of paper he had used to make a list before sticking it in his apron pocket. "I'll let you know what we can get."

"Thank you, Jacob. You are quite the salesman."

"Oh," he waved it off. "It's nothing."

"Well, I do appreciate you taking the extra time for me. Also, do you have any music?"

"Music? Like sheet music?"

"Yes. For piano."

"I think we might have something…" Jacob walked to the back of the store, passing by stacked bags of flour, sugar, meel, and wax-sealed jars of honey and preserves, before finally coming to a dusty pile of papers. "Here we are," he said, blowing the dust off. "I hope you like *Chopin*," he said, reading.

"I do, in fact."

"Very good, because that's what we have. Here, you can take them all."

"Are you sure? Thank you, Jacob. How much do I owe you?"

"Nothing, my new friend, nothing at all. They have been sitting here for more than a year. My father will be happy to know we're rid of them."

"Glad I can put them to use."

"Truth is, he's been wanting me to clean things up around here. I just haven't had it in me to throw them away. Something in me felt sorry to do it. Well, suppose I know why now."

Elliott tipped his hat and turned to leave. "I

really can't thank you enough."

"Listen!" Jacob called. "There's a carnival coming in a week or so, a group from Pottsville. Should be a good show. My father doesn't let me go, so I usually wait till nightfall to sneak out."

"My uncle likely would not permit it either. But it does sound fascinating."

"Most of the time it is. Maybe I'll see you there."

"Absolutely. See you, Jacob."

When Sunday came, the morning was perfect. Verdant buds shot out from tree branches. The sky was clear-blue and the air felt comfortable on the skin and light and easy to breathe. For the first time in a while, Elliott found the carriage ride pleasant.

"Beautiful day today," he said to his uncle. Other than Sterling, who drove them, they were the only two present. Charles never attended services.

"It is. Riding has always been enjoyable to me. Most people don't like it. It makes them anxious. But I find it relaxing. Most of my sermons are devised while I am riding or out waiting in the middle of a hunt."

"Really?"

"Yes, indeed."

"May I ask what this week's sermon is about?"

"Sure. Why not?" He removed his reading glasses and uncrossed his legs. "It's about Sodom and Gomorrah. How we human beings forget that God is always around us. Despite our ability to overlook his presence, he will abominate vessels of greed and lust should they take their hunger too far."

"I see."

When they arrived at the church, Levitt entered through a small door at the back, while Elliott went through the front doors like everyone else. He knew he would have to sit close to his uncle, but he wished he could sit at the very back so he could see Cecilia if she was there.

He kept his eyes aimed at the door until nearly everyone had arrived. When he saw Cecilia, she and her brother and sister were taking their seats in the very back. His heart pumped wildly. While the intense sensation would have normally made him panic, at that moment, he could not recall ever being happier.

"Good morning, ladies and gentlemen." Levitt began.

"Good morning, Reverend."

"This week is special, my fellow faithful followers. My nephew is joining us. He and his father have come to live with me and enjoy Gold as we all do."

Elliott could not help but blush. The attention of the entire room was on him.

"Elliott, please stand up." His knees felt weak, but he forced his legs up.

"Thank you," he turned, locking eyes for a moment with Cecilia. He willed time to stand still.

"You can sit down now, Elliott." His uncle and a few others let out a reprise of staggered snickers. That made his face really red. He was just happy he was in one of the first pews, so only a few people could see him from the side, and most of them were old and falling victim to senility.

After services, Elliott tried to catch up with Cecilia.

"Cecilia!" He called. "Cecilia Mason! Wait!"

"There's no need to yell!"

"Right, of course. Well, why didn't you stop?"

"I didn't want my sister to see," she whispered. Ruby had taken Caleb and gone ahead. When Cecilia looked in her direction, she saw the expression on her face was a mixture of confusion and contempt.

"Sorry. I just wanted to say hello."

"Hello, then."

Cecilia turned to leave.

"Wait! I want to ask you something."

"What is it?"

"There is a carnival coming to town, and I was wondering if you would like to go with me next week?"

"I doubt my sister will allow it but I'll ask."

"Well," he whispered in her ear; his body so close she could smell the boyish scent of his breath, a subtle hint of fresh air and pine with a touch of brown sugar and oats lingering from his breakfast. "I wasn't going to tell my uncle, either. Maybe we could keep it a secret. Just between the two of us. I'll come to the creek tomorrow at noon. Okay?"

She stood back, looking at him once more. A wave of heat inundated her body. "Are you sure?"

"Absolutely."

"Very well, I'll meet you there."

He picked up her palm in his hand. She thought he was going to kiss it, but he let it go at the last minute.

"What was that about?" Ruby asked as soon as she caught up with them.

"What do you mean?"

"Why was Reverend Eastman's nephew talking to you like that? Do you know him?"

"Not really. But he's nice. And maybe I'd like a friend other than you and Caleb. Maybe I'd like to *get* to know him."

"Oh, Sissy Mason," she rolled her eyes. "You better be careful…"

"Why?"

"Because people like the Eastman's and people like us don't go together. Besides, I doubt his uncle would ever allow it and neither would Pa."

"You know I never cared what men like them think. And I ain't about to start."

CHAPTER 12

It was difficult getting away from Ruby and Caleb. But, before noon, Cecilia left the house unseen to meet Elliott by the creek as she had promised.

Dipping her feet in, she could feel the water had warmed significantly. Reflections of the sun spanned across its surface, where the trees opened up to reveal the sky. When she heard someone coming, she shot up.

"Elliott?"

"Cecilia!"

They stood smiling at each other from opposite sides of the creek.

"I'll be right over!" she called.

"No!" Elliott said as he began to remove his shoes. "I will come to you."

"Okay." Cecilia stepped into the shallow part of the water, walking to the isolated island of land in the middle where the water split into two smaller streams on each side. "It's not too deep over here!" She told him. "If you cross here, you won't have to get your pants wet if you pull them up high enough!"

"Good enough for me," he said, pulling up his pant legs.

"The water isn't even cold!"

"Summer is coming."

"Yes, but I thought winter would never leave. It's actually starting to warm up some." He undid the cuff buttons of his linen shirt and rolled up his sleeves.

"Well, that's what Pennsylvania is like. You'll get used to it."

When he reached Cecilia, he nearly lost his footing, slipping on a rock. Without thinking, he threw his arms around her, trying to steady himself.

"Sorry," he said. "Can you stay long today?"

"Afraid not. I promised Ruby I would be back before nightfall to help her with dinner."

"I understand. Have you thought about the carnival next week?"

"You know I want to go. But how?"

"I will meet you here after everyone is asleep, and it is completely dark. I believe I can find my way in the dark," he quipped.

"Do you know where the 'Four-Points' fields are?"

"The what?"

"It's where the carnival is going to be held."

"Oh, I guess I hadn't thought of that…"

"Don't worry about it. I know how to get there."

"Great! I'll meet you here at half-past eleven then. Do you think that will be too late?"

"Not at all. The carnival goes all night." She looked at him for a moment. He was breathtakingly handsome; he seemed taller in the few months they had known each other; more muscular, and grown. "The country has changed you, Elliott. You seem different. More like a man, more grown somehow."

"You think so? I've been chopping some wood behind the house. My uncle doesn't know it, but I tell the stable boy, Thatcher, to leave me some from time to time."

"Is that your secret?" She smiled.

A strange look entered his eyes. Before she knew it, he was picking her up, plunging them both underwater. They came back up, his dark hair sopping wet.

"Now my clothes are soaked!"

"So are mine!"

"But I have to face my sister, Ruby. Now she'll know I've been up to something."

"Tell her you've been with me."

"You know I can't do that, Elliott."

"Why not?"

"Because, she'll be cross with me. I'm not supposed to be with you. Especially alone…"

"I see."

She helped him out of the water, his trousers and shirt drenched. "See you soon, Cecilia." He put his arm around her shoulders and brought her into his chest, placing a soft kiss on her damp forehead. He could taste the creek. "Goodbye."

Cecilia closed her eyes, wanting the moment to last forever.

CHAPTER 13

"Ms. Hakes? Could I talk to you for a minute?"

Elliott waited after school to speak with the schoolmarm. They were the only two remaining in the one-room schoolhouse.

"Elliott?" she looked up from her reading glasses. "What a surprise. Is everything alright?"

"Yes, ma'am."

The fair-haired teacher set her quilled pen down on her desk. "Well, you have my attention. What can I help you with today?"

"I know that I have only been here a couple of weeks so far, and that I was behind when I started, but I was wondering if there is a way I could apply to university early?"

"You'd like to go to university?"

"Yes, ma'am."

"Well, that's a little different from what I normally hear from students around here. What would you like to study?"

"I would like to become a doctor. After my mother became ill, it was my only wish to make her better. I always believed if I were a doctor, I could have done something more for her, as I may go on to do for others."

"Well, I suppose if you'd like to go to school, you could begin preparing for your entrance exams. I can't take class time to help you, but I can give you the right materials to help prepare on your own."

"Thank you, Ms. Hakes!"

"Are there any universities you are interested in attending in particular?"

"Well, my father went to Harvard, but I suppose anywhere would be fine."

"The University of Pennsylvania may have something of interest to you. I will write to a gentleman I know there, a professor. He may be able to give us information regarding any further requirements."

"Thank you, Ms. Hakes! I appreciate your help."

"You're intelligent, Elliott. It makes me happy that you wish to take your education further. As I said, most children around here cannot afford to go to school, let alone finish and attend college. That is a special thing, Elliott."

"Oh, I am most certainly not…"

"You are an exceptional young man, and don't you convince yourself otherwise. I'm sure your uncle Levitt sees what I have come to see in the short time we've known each other, and will be willing to help, too. When the time comes."

"My uncle doesn't know, Ms. Hakes. If you wouldn't mind, I'd like to keep this just between us. It's time for me to become my own man, apart from my uncle *and* my father."

"Certainly, Elliott. You may think I don't understand but I do. Your wishes are safe with me."

When Elliott walked home, he took the way Cecilia had taught him, past the general store and into the woods behind Lyman Steele's house; then northwest through the hills for two-and-a-half miles before reaching the fields, and then the gravel road leading to his uncle's estate.

"Elliott! Elliott! Wait!" He hadn't gotten far when he heard the voice of Jacob Miller calling him.

"Jacob! What are you doing here?"

"I was waiting for you to go by today when school let out." No one was around.

"It's awfully warm to be standing out here today, don't you think?"

"It is," he said, wiping the sweat from his brow. "But it's just as insufferable up in that old store. Anyways, my Pa's got it handled for the day."

It was an incredibly hot day. The sun burned in the wide-open afternoon sky. People sat inside or in sparse spots of shade. Dogs lay on their bellies in the dirt beneath porches in a futile attempt to cool off. Their tongues heaved as they panted without relief. Cicadas spanning from the tops of the trees screamed cacophonously.

Even Jacob, who was typically dressed in proper button-down vestments, had his sleeves rolled up, his shirt crumpled and stained by varying patches of perspiration. "I wanted to see if you planned on going? To the carnival? Like we talked about?"

"Please don't tell anyone, but yes, Sissy Mason and I plan to attend together."

"That's wonderful! What about her sister?"

"Her sister Ruby?"

"Do you suppose she would want to go too?"

"I can't say. Cecilia wasn't going to tell her because she didn't want Ruby getting mad and stopping her from going."

"Oh, I see," he said, disappointed.

"She's also the only one at home most times to watch their brother, Caleb."

"Yea, I wouldn't suppose James Mason spends too much time up there with his children."

"As far as I've been told, he doesn't—only when he needs something."

"Well, maybe some other time then. I do find Ruby to be a very pretty girl. I see her in church sometimes, sitting with the boy and Sissy. They are an unfortunate bunch, but I imagine some people just can't help what kind of luck follows them around."

"Luck can change though, Jacob. It can for you as much as it can for me. You'll see. I'll make sure you get your time with Ruby."

"You'd do that? Thank you!" His face lit up.

Later that night, Elliott struggled to sleep. He kept thinking what the carnival would be like. Would they ride the big wheel or carousel, or would a fortune teller divulge all life's mysteries to them for the price of a dime?

It was also unbearably warm. Even though all the windows were open, there wasn't a breath of wind coming through them. He sat up, sliding on his slippers as he headed to the window. The stars and moon were bright. The sound of the crickets in the fields droned on, persistent.

Although he would be meeting Cecilia the very next day, he decided to abscond once more to the creek for a night swim. He put on his pants and shoes and closed the doors behind him quietly.

Unfortunately, he had to go by Sterling's room, which was just down the hall. Tip-toeing and holding his breath, he made his way through the massive house in the blinding dead of night.

A branch poked him in the eye once he reached the forest; he almost tripped several times along the way. But, after several minutes, he was finally there.

He was not alone. In the light cast down into the clearing by the moon, there was Cecilia wading waist-deep in the water.

"Cecilia!" He whispered, trying to attract her attention. "Cecilia!"

"Elliott!" Her head snapped back. She struggled to see him between the trees in the dark. "Step forward, into the light, so I can see you."

"Okay."

"And why are you whispering? We are the only two out here. You can be sure of that."

"No, I know. I just didn't want to startle you."

"Alright then," she laughed. "What are you doing out here so late, anyway?"

"I couldn't sleep. You?"

"Same."

She lifted her arm into the air and brought it down with a splash. "This is as deep as it goes, right here."

"Where you are standing?"

She nodded.

"The water-level has gone down some since we first met here, hasn't it?"

"People are worried."

"Why?"

"The weather's been strange lately…"

"Why would that concern them?"

"Because they think it's a sign of something bad to come."

"Like what?"

"I don't know. Just something bad."

"Are you wearing anything, Sissy?"

She moved her hands back and forth on top of the water, tracing oblong ovals. "No. But it's because it was so hot. Besides, I didn't expect anyone else to be here…"

"It's alright. You don't have to be embarrassed. *I* should be embarrassed."

"Why?"

"Because I shouldn't just help myself to your creek, for one…"

"Relax, Elliott. It's alright. You can get in with me. You don't scare me." She moved closer to him. "I trust you."

"Maybe you shouldn't."

"Why? Do I have a reason not to?"

"No, but what if I were someone else?"

"But you're not. You're *you*. So, get in the water!" She splashed him.

"I suppose it's okay. If I just get in for a minute."

Cecilia turned and dove head-first, doing a somersault into the deepest part.

"Ah!" She gasped as she came up for air.

When he got in, the water felt warmer than the air.

"Barely does anything at all, does it?"

"What's that?"

"The water. It's *so* warm. It's like being in a bath."

"It's still better than nothing. You'll feel much better when you get into bed tonight."

"You're probably right. But I don't even feel like I'm getting wet." He cupped his hands, pouring water over his head and shoulders. Cecilia went to help.

"Why don't you just put your head under like me?"

He closed his eyes and threw himself into the tepid creek head-first as Cecilia had done. The water was dark, except for the very top, where the moon glittered subtly on its surface. When he came back up, Cecilia was gone.

"Cecilia!" He called out, trying not to panic or make his voice too loud. "Cecilia! Where are you?"

She bobbed up, laughing and gasping from holding her breath. "Did I frighten you?"

"Yes! Don't do that!"

She came over to him, slowly, reaching out to touch him with her open palm. "Your skin is softer than mine, but I like it."

"I like *you*."

For a moment, they were silent. They stood face-to-face. Mere inches apart in the water. Cecilia turned away to get out but he couldn't help himself. He had to kiss her. He reached for her, bringing her back in an embrace.

They remained this way for several moments, Elliott pressing his chin into the top of her head with immense intensity, like if he should let go, the world would end or time itself would implode. But, he knew it couldn't last forever.

"I should get going." she said.

"I don't want you to…"

"I wish we could stay here all night."

"One day, I promise, we will spend all of our nights and days together."

CHAPTER 14

Adam Vanguard knew he couldn't let his younger brother Alex go to the Masons' again. The first time he'd gotten nowhere. Adam needed action. He wanted to buy the Masons' land before anyone else. According to the geologist they had hired to study the area for oil, the Masons' plot of land showed the most potential for lucrative oil deposits.

Cecilia answered on the first knock.

"Good afternoon, my dear."

"Can I help you?"

"I am looking for a Mr. James Mason."

"I'm sorry, but you missed him. May I ask who's calling?"

"Name's Adam Vanguard. You may have met my brother not too long ago, Alex."

"Oh, the nervous gentleman who isn't too confident with his words?" Cecilia saw a resemblance in their face. But this man had darker features with a leaner, less muscular frame.

"That would be him. May I ask when you expect your father to return?"

"I don't owe you an answer, mister. But to make this short, I'll tell you: we don't ever expect him to return. What exactly is it you all want, Mr. Vanguard? Why have you all been coming around here?"

He raised one eyebrow before countering her question. "And, I'll be brief, my dear. I wish to offer your father money for this land."

"Why?"

"New things are happening all around us every day. Not that it means much to you, but men intend on drilling for oil right here, in Gold, beneath the earth. It's going to make many men rich practically overnight."

"Why do you want this property then? Why *this* one?"

"That is nothing you need to concern yourself with. Just know that I intend to offer you and your family a generous sum of money for it."

"Who's at the door, Sissy?"

"No one, Ruby. Stay inside."

"How old are you, Sissy?"

"My name is Cecilia. I'm thirteen."

"Well, my, you are astute for a child."

"I'm not a child, Mr. Vanguard. The fact is, you can't purchase this property."

"I won't stop until I have my way. So, I suppose that is all for now. Good day, Ms. Mason." He kicked his heels into his horse, pushing up dirt as he left back over the hill. "Yah!" He yelled, riding away. "Git!"

"Cecilia? Who was that?"

"It was Adam Vanguard. The brother of the other man who stopped here."

"What did he want?"

"They both want the same thing. They want to buy our land."

"I can't believe it! Why would they want to do such a thing?"

"He says they think there's oil here."

"*Oil?* What's that?"

"It's that black stuff that comes up out of the

ground. John showed it to me once."

Caleb came running around the corner to Cecilia's side.

"Hi, Caleb. Go get ready for bed, okay?" He obediently nodded. Cecilia pushed the front of his hair to the side. *"I love you."* She couldn't remember the last time she'd said it. "I'll go talk to John," she said, turning back to Ruby. "He'll know what to do."

CHAPTER 15

The next night, Cecilia and Elliott met beside the creek once more. This time, it was not for a swim but to go to the fields where *Marrow's Magic & Mysteries Co.* had set up their tents. Although the carnival came to town every year, Cecilia had never been.

Elliott wore a simple linen shirt with brown trousers.

"May I hold your hand?"

"Go on ahead." She laughed.

"Alright," he smiled. "Next time I won't ask."

"Here," she grabbed his hand. "Now you won't have to."

They walked through the woods together. When they reached the road outside of Gold, Cecilia stopped.

"What's wrong?"

"I don't really want to go there."

It was behind Lyman Steele's house. Although it was covered by the crisscrossed branches of several treetops, Cecilia could see a faint light shining from the middle of his house.

"Who lives there?"

"Lyman Steele," she said with a shudder.

"The taxidermist?"

"Yes."

"My uncle's taken plenty of animals to him. He's even been to the house a couple of times."

Cecilia thought of her proposed marriage to such a man and what her life would be like were she living in that house with him.

"Sissy? Are you alright? You don't look well. Do you need to go back?"

"No. I can do it. I just felt dizzy for a second. Must be the heat. Let's keep going. I'll be fine."

They walked behind the house. Cecilia wanted to yell and shout at her unseen tormentor, but she stayed silent and close to Elliott.

When they got near, they saw a sea of lights. People walked in a general ambulating mass arm-and-arm with one another, laughing and pointing at the exciting exhibits and exotic attractions they passed. Performers laden with makeup and ruffles rushed from place to place. Characters of a surreal show, there were voices everywhere.

"What would you like to do first?"

"I don't know," she said in awe. "There's so much here."

"What's that?" It was hard to hear each other over the throng of blurry murmurs.

"Come one! Come all! To see the amazing Roland and the stunning Esme! You won't believe your eyes, folks! See a man catch an actual bullet between his teeth!"

"It can't be real?" Elliott said as they passed.

"There's only one way to know!"

"You want to go?"

"Do *you*?"

Cecilia didn't know what to want. The carnival was already proving to be a strange place.

But then, a sudden rush of something

unexpected came over her: the desire to experience something new. A need to revel in every second of their night, to live in the here and now.

"Let's do it!"

"You're sure?"

"Yes!"

Her eyes lit up with excitement. Elliott was thrilled.

They waited in line behind others wanting to enter the gold and red striped canvas tent. Elliott took Cecilia's hand, not wanting to let go.

When they were inside, and everyone had taken their seats, the same announcer from outside began to speak again; his lips barely visible through his thick beard and curved mustache.

"Welcome one! Welcome, all! To the greatest show in history! This will be the most spectacular event you ever witness in your lives, folks! We ask those who are extra sensitive to move away from the front," he pointed. *"This is not for the weak of heart, folks!*

"Alright then! Without further ado, introducing the stars of the hour: Mr. Roland Kerr and Ms. Esme Snyder!"

The audience clapped.

"As advertised, folks, Roland and Esme are about to perform a feat never before attempted on stage! You've heard of William Tell... Well, this is even more daring! Prepare to be astonished as Roland attempts to catch a bullet between his teeth! That's right, folks! He will stop this penetrating piece of steel pushed by a powerful and explosive propellant with his very own teeth!"

Esme walked to the center of the arena and picked up a palm-sized revolver on a wooden stool. Her plum-colored lips and dark, cat-like eyes did not move.

Gripping the barrel of the gun with both hands, she stood with it pointed at her partner.

"She must have good aim," Cecilia whispered.

"I'll say..."

Roland took ten steps backward before putting both hands down at his sides.

"Roland," the announcer roared. *"Are you ready?"*

He did not say a word. He nodded his head one time up and down before looking straight ahead into the eyes of the woman controlling his fate.

"Please show the audience that you have nothing hidden." Opening his mouth, he revealed large square teeth with nothing between them. The entire crowd held their breath, unsure of what would happen next.

"Very well. Esme, take aim." She did. *"And fire!"*

People flew back in their seats when the bullet was released. Smoke filled the air. At first, it was hard to see what was happening, but then the gray mist cleared.

"Ladies and gentlemen," the announcer went over to Roland who was still standing. *"I present to you, the death-defying, Roland Kerr!"*

Roland spit the hot lead into the announcer's hand. "There you have it, folks!" He held it up in the air between his thumb and index finger, moving it around in a circle so everyone in the audience could see.

"Do you think it's real?" Elliott whispered.

"Don't you?"

"I'm not sure. It's all a little unbelievable. Wouldn't the bullet shatter your teeth?"

"Sh!" A hairy, older man sitting in front of them turned around. "Be quiet!"

"Oh, get on with yourself! The show's over anyway! Come on, Elliott." They were still holding hands, not letting go. "Want to go somewhere else?"

"Sure. Wait a minute! Look over there!"

"What is it?"

"Get down!"

"Why?"

"Do you see that big man walking over there, with the white shirt and walking cane?"

"Farmer Miller!"

Both knew that if he saw them, he would surely tell Elliott's uncle.

"What do you suppose Jacob's dad is doing here without his wife or children?"

"I don't know," Elliott answered. "But we should follow him to find out."

"What if he sees us?"

"He won't. We'll stay hidden. Do you think Jacob's here?"

"I think we should leave them both alone."

"What about the truth?"

"What if the truth isn't any of our damn business?"

"It's Jacob's business."

"Oh, fine. Just don't go getting me in any

trouble, Elliott. I mean it."

"I wouldn't do that. I promise."

They rushed past several others, following Farmer Miller before he disappeared into the darkness of an alley between two tents. For a few seconds, they waited in the shadows, until he appeared again. That's when he went to the door of what looked like an ordinary log cabin, but it was on wheels. He knocked with his cane.

A painted-up redhead with an emerald-green dress and a crooked stance answered.

"Can I help you, handsome?" She said with a coquettish grin as she pulled him inside by his suspenders.

"I think I've seen enough," Elliott said, walking away from the row of tents. "I have to tell Jacob about this."

"No, Elliott. Don't."

"Why? Don't you think he has a right to know what his father is doing? It isn't right!"

"My father does the same thing, and I don't like to hear about it. And I don't like to know about it."

"But maybe Jacob's not like you!" As soon as he said it, he regretted it. "I'm sorry, Sissy. That was wrong of me to say."

"We'll keep it a secret between the two of us. That way it won't be your burden alone to bear alone."

"Thank you, Sissy. Should we do something else before we leave?"

"Like what?"

"Anything you want."

"I think I would like to see a fortune teller."

"I thought you didn't believe in that?"

"I suppose it would be nice, you know? To find a way to communicate with her again–*my mother.*"

"Alright. Let's go."

When they found it, the black canvas tent was so dark on the inside, it was like it had no walls at all.

"Hello?" Elliott peeled back the tent's flap. "Is anyone here?"

"You may enter," an older female's voice answered.

"Please," she said, gesturing to the chairs before them. "Sit and tell me your names."

"I'm Cecilia Mason."

"I am Elliott, Elliott Eastman."

"They are strong names. You both come from strong families."

"Can we ask you questions?" Cecilia asked.

"First, I will tell you what I see. And then, you both may ask one question each. Understood?"

They nodded.

"Let me start with you." She turned to face Cecilia, setting a deck of cards in front of her. "Draw three and place them next to each other on the table, from left to right." Cecilia did as she was told. "I see," the woman exhaled deeply. "You were close with your mother. But she is no longer in your life. Correct?"

"That's right."

"But, why is it you come here tonight? Are you the one that wishes to speak with your mother?

Or, is it you?" she said, addressing Elliott. "Aren't you both out late for your age?"

"I am nearly seventeen."

"Well, with a sweet, innocent face like that, I should say…"

He frowned. She saw him. "Don't let my words be misheard, dear. You are a handsome one at that, without putting a second thought to it. Now, take the cards and shuffle them, and then turn down three as I've just told your friend to do."

"You two have the loss of your mother in common." She drew an invisible line between them. "Perhaps you've found one another for a higher purpose—a very specific reason. Oh my…" She broke off.

"What is it?" Elliott shot up, concerned.

"How did you say your mother died, Cecilia?"

"I *didn't*. But she drowned during a flood. It was on Elliott's uncle's property, in fact—the Reverend Levitt Eastman—during a flood."

"Ah, yes," she said, as if coming to some epiphanic understanding. "Two lives, forever connected. *A fabric and its thread."*

"What about Elliott's mother? Is there anything you can see of her?"

"I'm afraid it's getting late, and I must shut my doors for now, children. However," she looked at Cecilia. "I have a feeling we may see each other again. If not in this lifetime, certainly one of the next."

"What do we owe you, miss?" Elliott asked.

"Nothing. Nothing today. Now you two be

on your way."

After they stepped out, they were immediately greeted by a man surrounded by a small crowd.

"*What if I told you, I have the cure to what ails you right here in this medicine bag? Step right up folks, and purchase Dr. Curios Magical Medicine Elixir. Headaches? Gone! Tremors? Never again! Not after you try this, folks. But hurry! These little treasures won't last!*" The man held the little bottle up, theatrically marveling at the viscous liquid inside.

"Have you ever tried it?"

"Absolutely not!" Cecilia answered. "That man is full of it. There's no way in the world that stuff cures anything."

"I think if someone is sick, they might try anything to be better again."

"I suppose. But, some things plain don't work, and people know it, but they still try to sell it and make money off of other people's misery and trust."

They left the carnival and headed home. Both quiet, reflective, silently piecing together the night and all the things they saw.

CHAPTER 16

The following Sunday at church, Cecilia saw Elliott. She could feel his eyes on her skin, turning it hot beneath his stare. She tried to hide her uncharacteristic excitement but found it difficult to remember herself at times.

She was surprised to see Jacob standing with her sister after services. "Jacob!" Cecilia exclaimed. "To what do we owe the pleasure?"

"I was just asking Ruby here if she would mind accompanying me to the cotillion at the Reverend's house tomorrow night. I know that it's short notice, but will you, Ruby? Go with me, that is?"

"If you're sure you would like to go with me, then yes, of course I will, Jacob!" She threw her arms around him. He spun her in the air. Other churchgoers dispersing looked at them, gawking. But Cecilia didn't care; not wanting to interrupt her sister's happiness.

"I wanted to ask you the same thing, Cecilia." Elliott lowered his eyes. "Will you go with me?"

"Your uncle will never allow it!"

"This is why I waited so long to ask you…"

"Perhaps we should leave these two alone," said Jacob.

"Wait a minute!" Ruby cried. "What about Caleb? Who will watch him?"

"My sister Beth could do it," Jacob offered.

"That's alright." Secretly, Ruby did not want Caleb to terrorize any of the Millers or cause trouble. If Ruby and Cecilia were away, he was liable to cut her beautiful, long blonde hair or run off. Both Ruby and Cecilia knew they could ask John Wolfe.

"Please don't let that be a reason for you not to come, Cecilia…"

"Where is he?"

"Who?"

"Your uncle?"

"He's gone directly to the rectory. Besides, I already told him I planned to ask you." His soft, kind eyes melted her heart.

"You did?"

"Yes. He wasn't exactly jumping for joy. But he eventually said that I could take you. I told him how much you mean to me…"

"Oh, Elliott. I'm just not sure this is a good idea.

"It will be fine. Trust me."

"What will I wear? What will Ruby wear?"

"Leave that up to me. I don't know if you're the same size, but I think I know where I can find a couple of dresses."

"Where?"

"It's a surprise."

After church, Elliott rode home in the carriage with his uncle.

"You certainly are becoming quite fond of that Mason girl, aren't you?"

"Yes, I suppose."

"Wouldn't get too close if I were you."

"Why not?"

"I've planned to send you to a seminary for

boys. And it isn't exactly close. It's a couple hundred miles away. Besides, she looks like her mother who was nothing but a jezebel."

"You would speak ill of the dead, uncle? A man of the cloth? *Judge not, that ye be not judged,*" he recited. "Besides," Elliott continued with indignation. "I'm not going to go to a seminary. I'm going to a university to be a doctor."

"We all have wants and wishes, Elliott. Some are granted and some are not."

"But I can't leave."

"You don't have a choice. I am your keeper now, boy. Not your father. He gave you over to me, remember?"

"That's not true!"

"It is! Don't be such a fool, Elliott."

"Is this all about Cecilia? Is that why you are sending me away?"

"No." He said sharply. "Now that's enough. We'll discuss this later."

"Yes, sir."

CHAPTER 17

Before Levitt built the manor on the hill, he had lived in the modest church rectory. However, he found its size insufficient, and the centralized location unideal. He did not want to be in the center of town where everything was seen.

When Elliott returned, he once again sought out Esther Loudermilk. He found her changing the sheets in a vacant bedroom in another wing of the house.

"Esther?"

"Yes?"

She turned to find Elliott standing by the door.

"Are you busy?"

"Well, dear, you know I'm always busy but that doesn't mean I don't have time for you. Here," she patted her hand on a cedar chest at the foot of the bed. "Sit down here and tell me what I can do for you."

"I need a dress."

"For you?"

"No," he laughed. "It's for Cecilia Mason and her sister Ruby."

"Oh dear me, you really have become quite taken with her, haven't you?"

"Yes." His cheeks turned crimson.

"I know just what you need. Come with me."

They walked to the opposite side of the house, to the eastern wing. It was close to his aunt's rooms.

"Before your aunt Emily's accident, she used these rooms." Esther opened a pair of deep mahogany doors similar to others in the manor. The floors and walls of the room were a deep red, almost burgundy bordering on plum, with gold trim.

"It looked this way when she was well."

"It's incredible," Elliott turned around, taking it all in. "Are these gold sheets?" He went to the bed. Esther followed.

"Yes. Both your aunt and uncle have quite extravagant taste. There are several things up in the attic that belonged to your aunt. No one uses them anymore. You're free to go through them if you'd like. I don't know if your uncle would mind or not. But, if you ask me," she lowered her voice, "he never seemed very sentimental. Oh dear," she grasped her chin. " I suppose I shouldn't say such things."

"It's alright, Esther. I know you mean well. If Levitt asks, I'll tell him I found it on my own."

"I do hate to propagate a lie."

"It's a noble lie, so-to-speak. It will be alright."

She nodded.

"Well, the dresses are over here," she walked past the bed to an armoire. Opening the doors, she peered around inside. "It's been a while since anyone's worn any of these. I'm not sure what condition they're in."

"May I look?"

"Absolutely!"

He took out a midnight blue gown with a lace bodice and ballooning bell-shaped bottom.

"I think this one is perfect for Cecilia."
"And still in magnificent condition!"
"I need one for her sister, too. Is that okay?"
"How about this one?"

She handed him a yellow dress similar in shape to the one he'd chosen for Cecilia, but instead of a lace bodice, it had a large bow in the center that trailed down the back.

"It's perfect, Esther! Thank you!"
"It's nothing, Elliott. I'm glad you're attending with Sissy Mason. And who is Ruby going with?"
"Jacob Miller."
"That's just wonderful. Really it is. The Masons' may have a bit of bad luck, but they're good people deep down at the core of it. They deserve to participate in the pleasures of life, same as everyone else."
"If I can help it, Esther—I want to make sure that Sissy Mason—and her family—never go without again. I want to take care of Sissy—of all of them. You never did say what happened to their mother. It would seem she died around the same time Aunt Emily fell into her condition," he said, realizing it for himself.
"Oh dear, I'm afraid you are right. It was that very day. Oh my, but there was a strange way he'd look at Laura Mason. I suppose I shouldn't talk so, but it would seem the two are related–your aunt's misfortune and the death of Laura Mason."
"What happened?"
"Well, as you know, he rode off after Laura when talk of the floods began," she shrugged. "He

told everyone Laura Mason got swept up by Gold Creek. That he tried to save her, but the water came up and took her away. Last thing he saw of her, she was holding onto some thistle weed. Said it was either her or Emily, that he could only save one life. It isn't much of a surprise that the life that he saved was his wife's."

CHAPTER 18

After Sunday, Cecilia went to John Wolfe's to ask if he could watch Caleb during the Eastman's cotillion. Unfortunately, he wasn't home. She knocked and knocked but no one answered. Amidst all the excitement, she had forgotten that John had left for Ontario to meet with trappers, and wouldn't be back for another three weeks.

She wanted to kick herself for being selfish and forgetting her friend's plans. She went back home, disappointed in herself.

"What's wrong?"

Ruby asked as soon as she came through the front door.

"I forgot that John's out of town."

She sat down at the table, dropping her head down on her folded forearms.

"What if we took him to Jacob's sisters after all? There are four of them, and his mother. They should be able to handle him."

Both girls looked at their brother who sat only a few feet away from them on the floor. His hand flew up and down against the back of a pan. He had no toys or other things to amuse him.

"He'll do fine. We'll talk with him. It can't be this way forever, Sissy. We can't never leave his side."

"Fine. But we don't have much time. We better go to the Millers' today and ask if it'd be alright."

"I suppose we shouldn't have said no to begin with, but very well. Let's go."

They began walking the three-miles to the Millers' farm. It wasn't too far from the Eastman's estate. Caleb came with them, walking with elongated strides as he swung his arms back-and-forth.

The Miller's had four girls. Jacob was the only boy and the oldest. After him, came Beth, short for Elizabeth; then Hannah, Becca, and finally, Olivia.

The first thing they saw when they got close was Jacob on some sort of machine in the fields. Cecilia doubted he could see them. He was pretty far. Ruby walked up to the front door of their two-story farmhouse and knocked. It was a beautiful property with acres of open land. Mr. Miller had inherited it from his father, who had also been a farmer and ran the general store.

"Hello?" Mrs. Miller answered, wiping her hands on her apron. She was covered in flour. Her blonde hair was in a low bun and a little disheveled. "Can I help you, dears?"

Ruby stood in front of Cecilia holding Caleb's hand.

"I'm sorry to impose something like this on you Mrs. Miller. But we were hoping to speak with you or Beth about watching Caleb during the Eastman's cotillion?"

"Of course, come on in. All of you. Make yourselves at home."

"Thank you."

"Beth!" She called up the staircase. "Beth! Come down!"

The young girl appeared in an instant; shy

yet present.

"Hello, Ruby," she curtsied, holding up the bottom of her pale-green, checkered dress. "Cecilia, Caleb." She paused to bow to them respectively.

Beth folded her hands in front of her as she spoke. She had model posture, her hair brushed and parted neatly down the middle, half tied back with a matching ribbon.

"I was hoping to discuss something with you, Beth."

"Shall we sit down?"

Ruby nodded. They all chose a chair around the kitchen table and sat.

"Can I get anyone anything?" Mrs. Miller asked. "Perhaps some cookies? We've been baking all morning."

Caleb shook his head.

"Alright then. You come with me dear and we'll leave these ladies be." She held out her hand.

"Are you looking forward to the dance tomorrow, Ruby?"

"You know?"

"Of course, I do! My brother has been walking around here for weeks talking about nothing else. He was afraid to ask you. Thought you might say no…"

"No. I would never say anything but yes to your brother."

"Good. I know he likes you and has for some time."

"Well, I came here to ask you if you would mind watching Caleb tomorrow night? It happens that Elliott Eastman has asked Cecilia to go as well, and no one will be left to see to him for that time."

"I would be happy to."

"Thank you, Beth! You don't know what it means to me—well—us."

"Of course. My mother and father said I was still too young this year to attend the cotillion, but next year, you will have to ask Becca," she grinned. "Because I *will* be going myself. I've got my eye on several different suitors." She gave a wink.

"It's just for tomorrow night. We swear it."

They were about to leave when they heard the front door. It was Jacob.

"Jacob," Mrs. Miller said. "A couple visitors are here for you and Beth."

"Really? Who is it?"

"They're in the kitchen. Go see for yourself."

He ran in, covered in sweat; his hair turned lighter from the sun. He wasn't wearing a shirt, just pants with overalls. One strap was up while the other hung by his leg.

"Ruby! What a surprise!" He removed a white kerchief from his back pocket and used it to wipe off sweat from his face. "What are you doing here? Is everything alright?"

She stood up. He rushed to her.

"Hello," Olivia approached Caleb who had returned with Mrs. Miller. He stared at her with his blank eyes. "What's your name?"

"His name is Caleb."

"Doesn't he talk?"

"No, he doesn't."

"That's funny!"

"We'll be looking after Caleb tomorrow night. We will make him feel welcome, won't we?"

"Yes!" Hannah and Olivia answered in unison.

"Wonderful."

"Thank you, again, Beth," Cecilia said.

"It's nothing. I'm happy to."

"Bye Cecilia!" Olivia called. "Bye Caleb!"

For the first time, in a small, almost unnoticeable way of communicating, Caleb raised his tiny fist into the air and gave a brief, spastic wave before turning his head down and walking away with his sisters.

CHAPTER 19

On the day of the dance, many in Gold, particularly those who were younger and going for the first time, eagerly counted down the hours until that evening.

"Are you ready, Elliott?"

"I think I am."

He had dressed in a black jacket with a black tie; his hair slicked back and pushed to the sides.

"Oh, my goodness!" Esther was taken aback.

"What is it? Do I look alright?"

"You look nearly ten years older than you did yesterday. I can't believe my eyes."

"I do hope that's a good thing…" he smiled nervously.

"Oh, it is. You look very handsome, Elliott. I mean it."

"Thank you, Esther."

"No need. So," she said, changing the subject. "You are going to pick up Jacob Miller first, correct?"

"Yes. That's right. I'll need to take two horses."

"How will you manage that?"

"Cecilia taught me. She says if you can, take two females, because they're less likely to fight each other."

"Really?"

"I don't know. I'm just going off what she tells me."

"Well I hope it works."

"Me too."

"You dropped off her dress yesterday, didn't you?"

"Yes. The girls already have them. Everything and everybody should be ready."

He smiled at Esther.

"Will you be there tonight?"

"Oh, no! I'm not very quick on my feet anymore. Mr. Eastman allows me to rest during the dance. He has for some years now."

After getting ready and speaking with Esther, he went to the stable. People there would be working late into the night fetching people and taking them home. So, he helped himself to an all-white mare as well as a black one. He was not used to tacking up his own horse, but he had seen others do it countless times.

He polished two saddles and chose two bridles. The metal gleamed. Finally, he hooked a long lead-rope onto the black horse's harness, so that he could pull the animal along behind him. Their feet clicked on the black-locust wood floor.

"Giddy up, boy!"

They took off through the woods. Elliott only prayed they didn't get caught on anything, like a tree trunk or branch. When he reached a small stream, the white horse stopped dead in his tracks, throwing his head down.

"Come on, boy!"

But, the wrong horse listened to his command. Before Elliott realized what was happening, from the corner of his eye, a flash of black flew past. Still holding onto the black horse as it ran, he fell face-first into the shallow water.

After a few seconds, having a chance to regain his senses, Elliott stood up, spinning in a panic, figuring he had lost both horses. But, they stood in front of him, staring with indifference.

"Perfect!" He threw his hands at his sides. "Now I'm covered head-to-toe in mud! What am I supposed to do?"

He went to get the horses. This time, he decided, he would walk them to Jacob's, even though it would take longer to get there. It was too embarrassing to turn back.

"Elliott!" Mrs. Miller opened the door. "What's happened to you?"

"I fell, Mrs. Miller. Is Jacob here?"

"Jacob!" She called. "Elliott is here!"

Jacob came bounding down the stairs. "Elliott! What happened?"

"It's nothing…"

"Come on, dear. Why don't you go up to Jacob's room and find a change of clothes. It may not be as nice a suit as you were wearing, but we might have something like it."

"Thank you, Mrs. Miller."

"Just follow Jacob. He will help you."

"Come with me."

Luckily, nothing had gotten on his shirt or vest, so all he needed were pants and a jacket.

"Here you go," he handed him a black jacket from the trunk at the foot of his bed. "This looks like the one you had on. Now I just have to find some pants to go along with it."

"Thank you, Jacob. You are the closest friend I've ever had."

"Of course, Elliott. Until you came to town, I used to only have my sisters. There were no other older boys like us. Except for Kelsey Vincent, and he's always been a pigeon-liver who's too high for his nut."

"I know what you mean."

"Thanks for making changes around here, Elliott. Good changes."

"Well, I didn't mean too…"

"Sometimes you don't have to. Things just happen."

They went downstairs to show Mrs. Miller.

"Well! That suit doesn't look any different at all! You both look wonderful. Elliott, I will have that washed up and pressed for you in no time."

"Thank you, Mrs. Miller."

"No need to thank me."

The girls all sat in the main room around the fireplace; Hannah and Becca did each other's hair while Beth read Olivia a story.

"We'll be back with Caleb, Beth!" Jacob yelled from the adjacent room.

"There's no need to yell, Jacob," she said, coming into the room. "I'm right here."

"I know." He blushed.

"Oh, Beth! Leave him alone! He's just excited," Mrs. Miller chided playfully.

"Alright, Mama."

"We'll be back soon!"

"Wear your coat, Jacob! And try not to get anything on *you*!"

They untied the horses from the massive trunk of an oak tree beside the Millers' farmhouse and went ahead to the Masons' house.

When they arrived, the girls were dressed and ready to go. Caleb, too, knew tonight was different. He looked forward to being at the Millers' house. They had fun games to play and good things to eat.

To the girls, it was like a dream come true. Elliott and Jacob stood before them, dressed in elegance: the most handsome young men in all the town.

Jacob offered Ruby his arm. "Shall we, beautiful?"

"Of course." Ruby fixed her shawl as they descended the front porch. She looked back for a moment. The house was dark. A rare sight to see it completely empty at night.

Cecilia was nervous, but she could not wait to get away.

"You look nice, Elliott."

"As do you, Sissy. That dress fits you perfectly."

"It does. Thank you."

Cecilia was breathtaking. Ruby had pinned back her long dark hair so that her dark curls formed a braided band across the top of her head, while the rest hung down, reaching to her waist. Cecilia had brushed it a thousand times or more, wanting every curl to be soft for the occasion. To Elliott, her face was like a Roman Empress. The deep blue color of the dress complimented her olive complexion. To others, her beauty would be a surprise, as it was overlooked for so long.

CHAPTER 20

Elliott had not had many reasons to go into the ballroom before. But tonight, its opulence stunned him. Polished and lacquered, the wooden floors coruscated like gold. The chandeliers dripped from the ceilings like jewelry worn by kings and queens. Long tables of desserts and hors-d'oeuvres lined the south wall. Servants ambulated about with silver trays brimming with glasses of champagne and brandy.

They played several waltzes and a few songs by Stephen Foster and other composers, like Handel, Strauss, Chopin and Mozart. People whispered about the Mason girls being in attendance. Fortunately, there were more good words tossed around than not.

"Did you see their dresses? Wherever did they get them?" Judge Carlson's wife whispered into his ear. They walked arm-in-arm outside the dancing pairs.

"I don't know, dear. I would imagine the same place all young ladies purchase dresses..."

"How very cavalier of you. It *is* elegant. But, however did they manage to afford it? They look *expensive*..."

"Well, how about you ask her?"

"Maybe later," she said, veering to a table with desserts. "These look delicious! And *where* are those hors-d'oeuvres?"

Several individuals from town were in the band. Elliott was surprised when they began to play Liszt's *Love Dream*.

"This song is beautiful." He told Cecilia. "It is one of my favorites."

He placed his forehead against hers, but was immediately reminded not to get too close. From his purview, he could see his uncle glaring in their direction. Cecilia sensed it too.

"Maybe we shouldn't," she said, backing away.

"Forget about him."

"This is *his* home, Elliott."

"Well," his eyes came close to hers. "Let's not let him ruin this song—or tonight—for that matter."

She leaned forward, a coy, sideways grin on her face. "*Never.*"

She brought her arms closer around his neck. His cheek brushed hers, his skin slightly rough from his growing beard.

She looked at Ruby who appeared to be in a world of her own. She and Jacob were talking. Whatever he had said, made her laugh.

"Do you think they'll get married?"

"Who?"

"Ruby and Jacob?"

"Oh, certainly." He smiled, showing his wide set of straight teeth. "But I hope not before…"

"Not before what?"

"Not before I can ask you."

"Oh, Elliott. Please don't say such things."

"Why? There is no doubt you are the one I'd like to marry one day."

Their eyes met.

"Come here."

"What is it?" He was about to kiss her when the entrance of a man caught his eye, stopping him immediately.

"Who is that man who walked in?"

Elliott sighed. "That is my father."

"Your father?" Cecilia was shocked.

"Yes. He doesn't leave the stable loft most days. I don't know what could have made him come out tonight…"

"Maybe he wants to meet people."

"I don't think so. My father and people don't go well together."

"Why not?"

"It's a long story. I'll tell you about it later. Would you like to get Ruby and get going? I think I've had my fun for the night."

"I'm sorry you feel that way."

"It's not your fault. Nothing you do could ever make me feel as terrible as my father and uncle make me feel."

"You don't mean that, Elliott."

"I do."

"I'll go get Ruby."

When the four of them went to leave, Charles approached.

"Elliott," he said. "Aren't you going to introduce me to this young lady?"

"Father, this is Cecilia Mason. Cecilia, this is my father, Charles Eastman."

Charles took her hand, placing a kiss on top; his bifocals nearly toppling off. Elliott had never seen him display such an affectionate gesture.

"Very good to meet you, Mr. Eastman."

"And who is this?"

"This is Ruby, Cecilia's sister, and her partner for the evening, Jacob Miller."

"Oh, yes. *Miller*. That sounds familiar."

"My father owns the General Store, sir."

"Oh, yes! That's right."

Charles folded his hands behind his back, leaning forward.

"Headed somewhere, Elliott?"

"Yes, sir. Jacob and I are taking Ruby and Cecilia home."

"Sorry to have missed you."

"Me too, father." Elliott pushed past him. "Next time," he said, turning back.

"Elliott, was that your father? I've never seen him before. I didn't know he existed, to be truthful. Why didn't we stay longer?"

"The night isn't over yet, Jacob. Ruby, if it is alright, could I be alone with Cecilia for a while?"

She looked at them skeptically.

"There are a few things I'd like to discuss with her. That's all."

"Oh, fine. Just have her back home within the hour."

"Yes, Ruby. Thank you. Take whichever horse you'd like, Jacob, to take Ruby home. I can get it tomorrow. Keep it overnight."

"Are you sure?"

"Yes." Elliott put his hand on his friend's shoulder and locked eyes with him. "I thank you and Ruby for coming tonight."

"Until tomorrow then, Elliott. Come to the

house. I'll be using the combine in the fields. We've had lots of good growth after the rain. Sissy, if you can tomorrow, my dad and I could always use an extra pair of hands harvesting. And we'll be baling hay by the end of next week. This'll be our third and probably last time for the year."

"Of course, Jacob. We will be there to help."

"You're welcome to come too, Elliott, of course. There's some of mama's good home-cooking up for reward for anyone willing to help."

The Mason children had never tasted meats and pies like the ones Mrs. Miller made.

"Of course. Do you mind if we bring Caleb, too?" Ruby chimed in.

"That's fine. He can play around the house with the girls. Mama says they have really taken a liking to the little fella."

They said their goodbyes and parted ways. Little did they know, after that night, life would change for them all.

CHAPTER 21

Elliott and Cecilia took off from the dance on horseback. At first, Elliott had taken the reins. But, Cecilia preferred her way. He went too slow.

"Let me," she said, dismounting. They were about a mile from Levitt's now.

"Did I do something wrong?"

"No, here." She clicked her tongue and drove the horse into action. "Yeee-ahh!" They took off and Elliott's stomach lurched. He had never felt such excitement.

Leaves slapped against them as they raced through an intangible dark tunnel of forest.

"I've never gone so fast!"

"Would you like to go faster?"

"How is that possible?"

"Hold on!"

His arms went from grazing her ribs to squeezing them tight.

They pushed over the hill toward the Mason farm, veering just short of it. By the time they were done riding, nearly an hour later, Elliott had no idea where they were.

They got off the horse and lay on the grass in the open field. Stars stretched across the dark sky above them like a glittering web. The only sound was the chorus of crickets and a nearby barred owl.

"Elliott?"

"Yes?"

"Why does your father rarely come out of that barn? What is he doing up there?"

"It's hard to explain."

Cecilia propped herself up on her elbows and turned to him.

"Please…"

"Alright. He's a scientist and he's working for a man to refine oil."

"What does that mean?"

"About the oil?"

"Yes."

"He's making it to be used in homes. It has to be made different so it's safe. My father is working on getting the composition just right. He burns these fumes all the time. Truth be told, I resent him. I blame him for getting my mother sick and all those terrible coughing fits."

"That must have been awful. How did he end up getting involved with such a thing?"

"He was always a chemist of sorts interested in different compositions, but he was hired by this wealthy man recently to make it so it can be used as a source of energy of some type."

"Who is he?"

"Vanguard, something. It's a father and two brothers, but the father is too old to travel with them, so the brothers do most of the work."

"Vanguard." She repeated the name. "He's the one that stopped at the house!"

"Why?"

"Said they wanted to buy our house and all the land."

Something struck Elliott.

"What is it?"

"You must be that family I heard them talking about! Both brothers came over for dinner once, and they said there was a specific plot of land on the hill they were looking to buy. I never put it all together until now."

"Did they say anything else?"

"Oh, yes—Sissy, you can't sell that property. It's the best in Gold. One of the best geologists in the world came out and said so. I believe his name was Jasper, Jasper Cartwright. My dad and the Vanguard's discussed it at dinner. I'm telling you."

"Is that why you and your father moved here?"

"Yes." Elliott became embarrassed. "There was also an explosion, because of my father's work, in our tenement building back in the city. I blame him for that too. For us having to move. But, I suppose since I met you, it hasn't seemed so bad lately. People almost died, though. We were *not* welcome back. Uncle Levitt's is the last place he has left to go. Particularly if he's going to do the work he's set out to do." It was a sordid truth.

"Why don't the Vanguard's pay for him to have a proper place to do those things?"

"They offered to, and would, but my father, he is extremely averse to social settings and situations. He's somewhat of a hermit."

"You know what I wish?" she said.

"What is that?"

"I wish that we could always have this."

"What is *this*?"

"Our own world apart from everything and everyone else. A secret place made for *just the two of us*. That no one could ever buy or sell."

CHAPTER 22

The next day, they went to the Miller's house to help Jacob. It was hot. The sun burned their eyes as they walked in the open fields.

When they arrived, Jacob was already using the combine. The machine could be heard clanking and clattering for miles.

"Hello, Mr. Miller, Mrs. Miller." Ruby handed her a pie she had baked the night before. It had fresh blueberries and raspberries they had picked near John's house, just outside the Black Forest.

"What a beautiful pie, dear! Thank you. I'm just going to put it inside for now."

"What can we do, Mr. Miller?"

But he never got to answer. They were interrupted by an awful noise, a scraping and tearing of metal so awful; they would never be able to erase it or escape the memory.

"What was that?"

"I don't know."

Both Mr. and Mrs. Miller looked with worried expressions toward Jacob in the field and started running toward him, as did the others.

"He's not there!" Caleb screamed. "He's gone!" They were the first words he'd uttered in months.

Despite its chair being empty, the combine kept moving.

"Where is he?" Ruby shrieked. "Where did he go?"

"I don't know…"

Cecilia held onto Caleb who cried.

"What's wrong?" Beth came out of the house, the other girls standing at her sides. "What's going on?"

"I have to see," Ruby took off through the field.

"Ruby!" Cecilia called after her. "Ruby! Wait!" But it was too late. Ruby reached Jacob and collapsed, releasing desperate screams of despair.

Drenched like a blood-soaked rag, Jacob slipped away from life. He had tried to release something from the combine blades when it caught his arm and pulled him. His father tried to pick him up and take him back to the house, but it was too late.

CHAPTER 23

Moans of mourning emanated from the Masons' house for days. It arose from the loft and resounded throughout the fields. From the creek, it became a ceaseless faint echo.

Cecilia tried to get away as much as possible, despite feeling incredibly sorry for Ruby.

"Cecilia?"

"Elliott!" She waded through the creek to greet him at the bank. The water was low. Summer's heat had taken most of it, leaving behind several dry patches and protruding stones.

"What happened to all the water?"

"It's dried up."

"There's barely enough water for you and your family here, let alone enough to irrigate your crops." He squinted, looking at the sun as he wiped the sweat off his brow. "What are you going to do, Sissy? How are you going to water the crops?"

"I don't know. But that's the least of my worries. I can't get Ruby out of bed and Caleb doesn't know what to do with himself."

Elliott held his chin with his hand and rubbed the sides of his face. "I still can't believe what's happened to Jacob. I saw his mother and father again today. They're in a terrible state. Jacob's funeral is tomorrow. Are you going?"

"Yes, of course."

"And Ruby?"

"I'll try to see to it that she goes. It has been very hard on her. She's not eaten, slept, or done anything but cry for days."

Tears formed in the corners of Elliott's eyes. He squeezed them back, but one after another, they streamed down his cheeks.

"If—If—we would have shown up earlier…" he wept. "If—If—I would have been there sooner. None of this would have happened…"

"Elliott," she cradled his face, holding him against her. His sobs were stifled by her chest. "This is not your fault. It isn't my fault and it isn't the Millers' fault. An accident is an accident. There's no changing it. Even if we knew the way how. No one can go back. No matter how bad they wish they could."

"I don't know…"

He lifted his eyes to look at her. "I love you, Cecilia."

With her thumbs, she wiped the tears away from his eyes.

"And I love *you*, Elliott. I know it seems like things are very bad right now, but they will be better again. After Jacob's funeral, Ruby will need to mend, but she'll get through this. We got over our Mama's death, and we'll weather this too."

"This too shall pass." He gave her a weak smile.

"Yes. I suppose. It's just that I don't have a lot of help with the farm with Ruby this way."

"What about your Pa?"

"He's been gone for days." The sudden remembrance of her father made her heart plummet. "Elliott, there's something I need to tell you."

"What is it?"

"My father wants me to marry another

man," she blurted. "It's Lyman Steele."

"Lyman Steele? But he's so much older, and not very attractive, I might add.."

"My father has accepted some money from him and now says it can't be undone."

"Then I'll offer him more money. My uncle—"

"If you dare ask that man for money I'll never speak to you again!"

"Why not?"

"Because, he's always treated me rotten, and you'd be the only reason he'd want to help at all. It's—it's just not right…"

"Fine. I'll get *my own* money. How about *that*?"

"Elliott, you can't be serious. But how?"

"You don't believe me?"

"I do! But, it's not just about you and me anymore. It's about my sister, and Caleb. I can't have them getting hurt because I ran away or disobeyed…" Her eyes pleaded with him. "Don't you understand?" She began to cry. "It's not just about me. My brother and my sister need me."

"Believe me, Sissy. I'm not letting anyone or anything come between you and your family. It's just the opposite. Here," he said, stepping back to remove something from his pocket. "I want you to have this."

"It's beautiful!"

"It's a golden locket. It belonged to my mother. I gave it to her a few days before she died. She never had a chance to put anything in it. It's always been empty but I hope to put our photographs in there one day."

"Thank you, Elliott!"

They embraced before he placed it carefully around her neck.

"I also want you to take this horse. I know you don't have one for your family any more. Just hold on for a bit longer, Sissy. And one day, we'll be together always."

"I'll do what I can."

The creek was too shallow to swim. No birds flew overhead. Where had all those quiet, unassuming things gone?

CHAPTER 24

Cecilia returned home that night to find her father at the kitchen table. A large jug of whiskey at his feet.

"Sissy Mason," he snarled. "Where you been at, girl? Been waitin' for you to turn up."

"Out by the creek, Pa. Crops are starting to get dry, and we don't have enough water to give them. Might have to build a well soon."

"You won't have to be worrying yourself with all that now."

"What do you mean?"

"Lyman's coming for his bride tonight." He smiled, revealing a square-shaped hole on the right side where his tooth had been punched out.

"But–"

"But nothing, girl. You ain't got nothing to consider so gather your things."

He got up to grab her, but Cecilia fought back. "You can wait outside," he said, as they wrestled. "You ain't welcome here no more!"

"Ruby!" Cecilia yelled up to the loft. "Ruby! Please!"

Ruby flew over the edge. "Papa?" she said, her eyes blurry and swollen. "What's going on?"

"Just go back to sleep now, darlin'. There ain't nothing for you to be worried about down here."

He got a hold of Cecilia's shoulder's and continued pushing her toward the door.

"No!" Ruby hollered. "You can't, Papa! Let Cecilia stay! Please don't do this! We *need her*!

Caleb and I *need her*!"

Caleb came running around the corner of the house and to the front door. He had been hiding in the barn the entire time.

"Don't touch her!"

James Mason was stunned by the sound of his own son's voice. He nearly toppled over. "What did you say?"

Caleb didn't answer. Instead he hauled off and kicked his father right in the knee.

"Yowwwww!" He howled like a wounded animal. "You children make me miserable! I'll get rid of each and every one of you, I will!"

"Run, Sissy!" Caleb yelled. But James Mason's wide, stout hand came down on Caleb's head. The force of the blow hurled his small body to the floor.

"Don't hit him!" Without hesitating, Cecilia threw her fist into the air toward her father's spiteful face. But it did not take him down. The punch merely irritated him.

"I'll get you!"

"Caleb! Sissy! Look out!" Ruby had pushed their chest of clothing to the edge of the loft. With a final shove, it came crashing down on James Mason's head. Just as he looked up, it fell, blackening his senses. One final breath escaped from his maw before he passed out.

"Sissy! You have to get out of here!"

Ruby came down the ladder.

"Here," she handed Cecilia a few silver dollars. "I've saved them. Take them and go someplace safe. Go to John's or Ms. Hakes's…"

"I can't, Ruby. He'll find me."

"Take the horse and go as far as you can with this." She closed her sister's hand over the coins. A loud bang came from the center of the room. Their father was getting up. He threw the chest aside. "Go!" Ruby screamed. "Get out of here while you can!"

James Mason tried to say something but all that came out was an incoherent garble. His hand reached up to hold his head.

"What about you and Caleb? You need to go too! He'll hurt you both when he finds out you helped me!"

"We'll leave too. Just go, Sissy! You can't let him catch you!"

Sissy gave her sister a final desperate look and dashed for the front door. It was the closest, and her father would be able to reach out and grab her if she used the back one.

He tried to lunge for her, but it was too late. She was gone. Before James Mason realized it, Ruby had taken Caleb and was running for the back door.

"Not so fast!"

This time, it was Ruby who kicked him in the knees. He went straight down.

"I'm going to kill you every last one of ya! All of ya!"

Once they were outside, Ruby put Caleb down. Both of them ran until they were deep into the forest. Out of breath, they sat at the trunk of a tree. It was getting late.

"What are we going to do, Ruby?"

"This is what we'll do. We'll stay here until morning. But keep your voice down. We don't want Papa to hear us."

"What about Sissy? How will we find her?"

"She won't have gone far. Now, come here." She pulled him into her side and arranged her skirts around them for warmth. "There. It keeps some of the wind out doesn't it?"

"Yes," he nodded.

"Good. Now, we'll just pretend we've been shipwrecked."

"Shipwrecked?" He craned his neck quizzically.

"Exactly. We've been thrown into some dark waters but come daylight, we'll be right back on dry land again. It won't be long. We just have to hold tight."

"I don't like this game, Ruby." He whimpered.

"Shh…" she tried to soothe him. "I know, Caleb. It will be alright. We'll go to John's or Ms. Hakes' house tomorrow morning, and we'll have a lovely breakfast. Would you like that?"

"Yes." He rubbed his eyes with the back of his tiny closed fists.

"Good. We have to try and sleep now, do you understand?"

"Yes."

She rubbed his forehead and kissed him on the cheek.

"I'll take care of you, you know that? I promise."

"I know, Ruby." He held tight to his sister as

they waited, alone, in the dark. The desolation of night and their despair closing in on them.

"I hope Cecilia is okay. How will we find her again? What if Papa finds her first?"

"We'll have to worry about that tomorrow, Caleb. Tonight, we worry about us."

CHAPTER 25

Cecilia rode through the night across the hills. She didn't sleep for days. Adrenaline sent her reeling, continuing ahead without thought of an end. Eventually, her horse grew weary, stumbling over a jagged rock. Cecilia desperately urged it forward, trying to stop it from falling, but the poor beast's limbs buckled and she went sailing forward. For a moment, she was grateful for the feeling of weightlessness. But, then she hit the ground.

The horse was fine. But she decided to take a break, confident she was too far outside Gold to be found by her father. She tied up her horse by the entrance of a cave. It was beginning to get hot, and even though the walls were damp, there was shade.

A while after she had fallen asleep, Cecilia was startled by a noise.

"Don't be afraid! Are you hurt?"

"No. I don't think so. Who are you?"

"Name's May Flower."

"Is that your *real* name?"

"Well, that's a rude thing to ask! What's your name?"

"Cecilia, Cecilia Mason."

"Oh, well, that's quite pretty…"

"Thank you."

"My real name is Lenora. May Flower's just my stage name."

"Your stage name?"

"Oh yeah. My family and I are part of *Marrow's Magic & Mysteries Co*. We travel all over. Have you heard of us?"

"Were you in Gold a few weeks back?"
"We were!"
"Where are we now?"
"You're in Hazleton."
"Hazleton?"
"You're from Gold?"
"Yes."
"And you made the trip overnight?"
"A day or so."
"We've been traveling for a while too, but we stop a lot in between along the way. Did you see us when we last came to Gold?"
"I did. It was quite spectacular. How did you find me, anyway?"
"Hawkley."
"What's a Hawkley?"
"He's the one who took your horse. Said it was a nice one."
"He did what?"
"He took it. I tried to stop him, though. Honest!"
"I see. Will you take me to him?"
"He's practicing right now. He's star of the dressage show."
"I don't rightly care, May."
"It's *May Flower*."
"Right, *May Flower*. A *thief is a thief*, and I'm getting my horse back."
"What are you supposing to do?'
"I'm going to get back what's mine, that's what I'm *supposing to do*."
"He ain't gonna like it."
"Take me to him now!"

"Oh, dear, come with me then."

It wasn't long before they came upon tents, not too far from where she'd been sleeping. She hadn't heard the noises from the elephants or pounding from the erectors or anything.

"You aren't gonna want to disrupt him." May Flower warned.

"And why not?"

"You'll interrupt!"

"He should a thought of that before he went ahead and stole my horse!" Cecilia said, storming off.

"Wait!" May Flower called. "Wait!"

"What?" Cecilia asked, crossly.

"Mr. Warby won't like it either—he won't like it the most!"

"And who's Mr. Warby?"

"He's the manager. He's the one who owns the carnival and tells everyone what to do. If you stop the show, and stop Hawkley from riding his horses, Mr. Warby will punish all of us!"

"Well, then, let me talk to him."

"You want to talk to Mr. Warby?"

"If he's the one in charge, then yes."

"Okay, then. But, I'm warning you, Sissy, he's not very nice!"

"Just lead the way and let's go."

They walked to one of the biggest tents in the ephemeral carnival arena. "Mr. Warby?" May Flower stayed behind the tent flap until she was beckoned to enter.

"What is it, girl?"

The rotund man with a mustache and glasses

concentrated heavily on a leather book filled with numbers in front of him.

"There's a girl here has some business with Hawkley."

"Oh, for goodness sakes," he took off his glasses and rubbed his forehead with the flat of his palm. "What's the boy done now?"

May Flower looked to Cecilia, who entered the room.

"He's stolen my horse, sir."

"Oh, that's all?"

She stared him down with unforgiving adherence.

"Yes, sir. That's all. But I would like it back now, *is all.*"

"Well, yes, of course. After the show tonight, I will have him deliver it to you personally. Where do you live?"

"Why, nowhere really, sir."

"Nowhere, really? And what does that mean? Have you no home? Are you an orphan?"

"Not exactly, sir."

"Mr. Warby, please, call me Mr. Warby."

"Yes, Mr. Warby."

"Very well. May Flower?"

"Yes, sir?" She approached them both, coming in from outside.

"Do you and your sister have extra room in your tent?"

"I suppose we could find another cot. There is Ms. Tzavaras. She may have, you know, the one from her son…"

"Ah, yes. Terrible what happened. Ask

around and see if you can find something." He turned to Cecilia. "You are welcome to stay here for as long as you'd like. We are a sort of family. We take care of each other and will take care of you for as long as you need."

"Thank you well enough but I'd just like my horse back and then I'll be on my way."

"Please, stay the night. I can tell by looking at you, that you have a lot of hidden talent."

"I don't think so..."

"Just say you will stay the night. What is your name?"

"Cecilia, Cecilia Mason."

"Beautiful. Stay as long as you'd like, *Cecilia.*"

"Thank you. But you will be sure Hawkley returns my horse, won't you?"

"Yes, yes, my dear—yes, yes. I will have it taken care of tonight. Just wait in May Flower's tent."

"Thank you, sir."

Cecilia was skeptical, but she decided to stay in hopes of having her horse returned. On foot, she would not be able to travel as far or as fast, and she would never get back to Gold without it.

CHAPTER 26

May Flower had a sister, June Bug. She wasn't as nice but she was just as pretty. Both had long hair they kept pinned up. However, instead of fair, blond hair, June Bug had sleek, black hair, even darker than Cecilia's.

"I don't understand why we have to take her in," June said as she sat in front of her vanity mirror, combing her hair.

"Because she is a girl about our age. Who else is she going to stay with?"

"Ms. Tzavaras is one child short, isn't she?"

"June Bug! How dare you say something so stunning? Really, sometimes…"

"What?" She looked back at her sister in the mirror, her hair curled and already set in place. "She *is*."

"You're awful."

"What happened to Ms. Tzavaras?" Cecilia asked.

"Her son passed away three years ago."

"How?"

"He drowned. Went swimming in a nearby hole and got sucked down by some kind of whirlpool. Nobody's quite sure how it got there. But he was a strong swimmer. Shocked everyone."

"That's awful."

"It was a very sad time."

"Oh, will you two quit talking like a couple of witless lunatics? It happened a long time ago. Time moves on and so do I," she said, her voice taking an icy tone.

"Your heart is cold, June. It makes you callous."

"And yours is too warm. It makes you *foolish.*"

"Oh, just finish getting ready. We'll be on soon."

"Will you be here when Hawkley comes?"

"I don't think we will, Sissy. But, I know you can hold your own. You'll get your horse back." She winked.

While the sisters were gone, Cecilia looked around their tent. Idle time passed slowly. She could not help herself. They had rouges, powders, creams, and even novel contraptions for keeping their hair in curls. A knock interrupted her observations. Most people, Cecilia noticed, used wooden boards tied to a post near the doorway that visitors could knock on to indicate their presence.

"Hello?"

A young blonde man with his hair tied back came in through the tent flap. He wore a loose, white shirt with ruffles around the sleeves and collar.

"Are you Cecilia Mason?"

"Yes."

"I tied him outside for you."

"Why did you take him?"

"Excuse me?"

"Why did you take my horse? You could tell he belonged to someone else."

"No, I did not think he belonged to someone else. He was standing alone in the forest. You were nowhere to be found."

"May Flower found me," she challenged.

"Listen, I didn't know he belonged to you! You weren't around! And I don't appreciate being deemed a thief."

Cecilia came close to him. "Either way, thank you for giving him back. I'll be on my way. Please tell June Bug and May I say goodbye."

"You're leaving? Why don't you stay and tell them yourself?"

"Because, I've got to get back home."

"Where's that?"

"Gold."

"Gold? Why, that's hundreds of miles away! How did you get so far?"

"That horse." She untied him and jumped on.

"Do you want a saddle or something?"

"No. I'll make do without it."

"You sure can ride…"

"Sure, good as anybody else, I suppose."

She turned around in a circle, not sure which way to go. The sun was gone, so she would need to find the North Star. Once she spotted the brightest star in the sky, she nudged her horse. Starting at a canter, she would go north, back to Gold.

"Good luck to you, Cecilia Mason!" Hawkley called. Cecilia continued gaining speed, not looking back.

When she reached the woods, something caught her attention. At first, she thought it was her imagination. But, upon further inspection, Cecilia saw something moving alongside her in the trees.

"Woo! Hoo!" She heard a man holler. She could see floating orbs from fire torches surrounding her on both sides.

"Looks like we caught us something big, boys!" She heard another man yell. Her heart began to pump fast. She willed it to slow down but it would not. Just then, the pounding sound of a horse's hoofs beating on the forest floor flooded her ears. *"Thuh-thud-thuh-thud-thuh-thud…"* It sounded like one person rushing to overtake the others. "You men get out of here!"

They roared with laughter in response. Just then, Cecilia saw Hawkley appear. He was the unaccompanied rider on horseback.

"Come with me back to the camp. You'll be safe there. I'll make sure of it."

"Do you know those men? Why didn't they try to hurt you too?"

"Because the outfit has an agreement with them. We don't bother them, and they don't bother us."

"Why not?"

His eyes narrowed. "Because they and Mr. Warby have an understanding."

She began to cry. Her head hung low, defeated.

"What's wrong, Cecilia? Are you okay? Have you been injured?"

"No, it's just that—It's beginning to really hurt. How much I miss my family and everyone back home." Her heart began to ache for Elliott and to see him again, to once again gaze into his loving eyes. "I feel terribly alone."

"You aren't alone. I'm here. And that's something you can count on—at least for now."

CHAPTER 27

Cecilia spent a lot of time with Hawkley for the next month. Until she could remember what shows were when and which performers did what. She waited long enough for the rough band of men that had confronted her to get long gone. Hawkley, however, did his best to convince her that she would never be safe outside of the carnival again.

She sat in front of the mirror in the tent she shared with June and May Flower. She had become fond of them both. Even June Bug with her dour demeanor. Both had allowed her to stay as long as she wanted.

Hawkley stood at the center of the tent, leaning against the wooden post. "You are safe here. I don't understand why you shouldn't just stay with us here at the carnival. Your own family back in Gold chased you out anyway…"

"Just my Pa, Hawkley. You're hardly being fair." Since she'd left Gold, Cecilia's appearance had changed in some ways. Her features had become less cherubic and childlike and more statuesque and refined. She put on a bit of rouge belonging to May and June. She secretly loved to experiment with their exotic things. "Besides, I have a life I need to get back to."

Without hesitating, he went to her. "What about me? I can be your life. We can start one together."

"I'm afraid I can't do that, Hawkley. I've already promised my heart to another."

"Ah, I see," he said, disappointed. "Well," he kissed the top of her hand. "I hope that we will always remain friends, Cecilia Mason."

"I do too, Hawkley. I couldn't have made it out here without you. You've helped me so much, saved my life even. I owe you a lot, and May and June too."

"I'm certain you would do the same for us."

"Cecilia," May came bursting into the tent. "I have something to tell you."

"What is it, May?"

"People around camp are saying that Mr. Warby is asking to speak with you."

"He is?"

She nodded.

"I suppose I better go then."

"Please be careful!" She urged.

"Yeah, perhaps I better go with you," Hawkley offered.

"No. I'll be alright."

"Keep your wits about you."

"I will, Hawkley, and thank you for letting me know, May."

She approached his tent. A dim light shone through the opening.

"Hello? Mr. Warby?"

"Ah, yes. Our newest member of the family. Come in and sit, sit."

"May said you wanted to see me?"

"That's correct. I wanted to see how you'd feel about doing a show?"

"What kind of show?"

"Any kind you're good at. That's usually

how it works..."

"Well, I was planning on heading back home in a short while here. I was hoping to earn enough money to get another horse somewhere. My old horse, the one Hawkley got off with—well, I can't deny Hawkley rides him well. It's a sight to see when they perform. I just don't have the heart to take it back now."

"I see, girl. And how were you planning on paying for that horse?"

"It would be a trade. But I can pay anything you deem necessary."

"Ah, yes. But the work you do around here barely covers your stay. I do think it's time for you to consider alternate ways to earn money, girl."

"But, don't I work hard enough? Don't I do what I'm supposed to?"

"Oh, yes. Why, of course, Ms. Cecilia. That's simply not what I'm getting at. You have me all wrong. It's just that it costs one quite a lot to be on their own. There's food and water, and it would appear you are also helping yourself to toiletries."

She blushed. "My apologies, sir. Perhaps it's best if I get on with it now."

He let out a contumelious chuckle. "Well, darling. I didn't mean to push you out. But, please, do as you must."

"Yes, sir. And thank you for welcoming me here and letting me stay and all."

"Come back any day, Cecilia, darling. Any day."

"Thank you, Mr. Warby."

"Yes, yes. Now go on back to whatever it is

you were doing."
    She nodded and walked out.

CHAPTER 28

Black rain fell over Gold that October. The people, like the water, felt the change hovering like an odd, oppressive fog.

Adam Vanguard stood with inky streaks coming down his clean-shaven face. He smiled. His plan to successfully drill for oil before the ground froze had worked. He was the first ever to achieve this feat.

"What did I tell you?" he said, pulling his brother to his side. The two slipped on the wet earth, leaning into each other for balance.

"Light that cigar, little brother!" he said. "We're about to be rich!"

Oil shot into the air, geysering with fury. The flame at the top of the rig ignited, setting off a significant blast. The ground quaked. "We've finally done it! Now we just have to make our way over that hill," Adam said, pointing right for the Masons' property. "But, tonight, we celebrate."

CHAPTER 29

After speaking with Mr. Warby, Cecilia went to Hawkely's tent where he stayed alone. She waited for him.

"Sissy? What are you doing here?"

"I came to tell you something."

"What is it?"

"I've decided to leave. I want to give you my horse. You ride so beautifully together. I was just hoping you could help me find another one to get by on."

"You won't need to," he replied.

"What do you mean?"

"I'm going with you."

"No, I can't ask you to do that. Your family is here. You've been here all your life. How could you *want* to go?"

"You've become a close friend to me, Sissy. I was hoping to go with you and maybe do something different for a while."

"I can't ask you to leave everything you know."

"And I don't want to see you travel all that distance again all alone. Let me go with you. If there isn't something for me there in Gold, I'm certain Mr. Warby will let me come back."

"Are you sure?"

"Yes. And that eliminates your problem of having to save money for a horse. We'll just have to save some for food and places to stay. It may be safer than the woods if we keep our money and belongings under a close eye."

"When should we plan to leave?"

"In one week. That will give us enough time to get everything in order. One last thing."

"Yeah?"

"You better tell June and May goodbye sooner than later. They'll be sorry to hear the news."

"At least May will. They'll be sorry to hear you're leaving too, Hawkely. Everyone will."

"Well, we better get our rest then." He turned to leave. "Goodnight, Sissy."

"Night, Hawkely. Wait!" She called. "One last thing: when I saw the carnival before, in Gold, there was a fortune teller. In all my time here, I haven't seen her once."

He laughed. "You're a funny one. But you can't put me on, Sissy. We haven't had a fortune teller here. Never have."

CHAPTER 30

Without Cecilia, the days were long and daunting for Elliott at his uncle's estate.

"I notice you aren't yourself lately, Elliott," Levitt asked one night while they ate dinner. "Is something wrong?"

"No, sir."

"Oh, come now." He wiped his mouth with his napkin before placing it back in his lap. "Lying is a sin," he wagged his finger. "This wouldn't happen to have something to do with the recent disappearance of the Mason girl, would it?"

"I suppose it does, sir." He tried to sound ambivalent, not wanting to delve too deep into the subject. But his uncle persisted.

"It's all for the best, rest assured, dear boy. She was like her mother. Trust me. I knew that Laura Mason more than you could expect. Evil in. *Evil out.* She's passed her ways onto those children, *especially that Sissy.*"

"It was you who helped her the day she died, correct?"

"It was an accident!" He blurted. There wasn't a thing I could do!" He stood up, throwing his chair behind him and his napkin on the table. "I think dinner's over. Go to your rooms, Elliott."

Elliott decided after dinner that he would leave his uncle's estate and save up enough money to find Cecilia. There was just one thing he had to do first.

He packed a few things, but before going to

the front door, he decided to pay his aunt Emily a visit. Hoping no servants were in the room with her, he quietly and carefully pushed the door open, but just a slight bit, peeking his head in to get a glimpse of the room, which appeared empty. He came to her side, taking her delicate, wrinkled hand into his own.

"Aunt Emily," he whispered. "It is me, Elliott. I am terribly sorry to disrupt you. I just wanted to say hello before I said goodbye." She felt him squeeze his hand tighter. It startled him.

She turned to him, her eyes filled with sadness.

"Elliott," her voice cracked. "My dear," she began to shake, her eyes filled with tears.

"But… but… I thought you couldn't speak! Aunt Emily! But it isn't true?"

She clasped both her hands as tight as she could, shaking. "You need to go! You need to get away from him now," she hissed.

"Who, aunt Emily?"

"*Your uncle*! He is a monstrous man. If the town knew what he did to that poor Mason woman…"

"What did he do?"

She looked around nervously. "I will tell you, dear boy. But don't repeat it. He will stop at nothing to keep his evil ways a secret.

"He said he was going to help her. But that's the last thing he intended to do when he took off for the Masons' that day. I saw him, on top of her. Then he saw me, with those wild eyes. That's when he pushed her in, right into the rising water. She clung for dear life to stop it, but he kicked and kicked at her until she let go and was swept away. They said she drowned. But I knew better. I saw it with my own eyes—it was my husband. He came after me next, hitting and striking me about the head, hoping I would forget," she let out a stifled sob. "But I remember *everything*, Elliott. *Everything.*"

Both of them paused when they heard the sound of Levitt at the front door.

"Go! Go now and don't tell anyone what I've testified to here today. Leave here now and swear to me you won't ever come back!"

"What about you, aunt Emily?" His eyes pleaded. "I will come back for you! I promise!"

"Keep yourself safe, boy. That's all I can ask of you." And with that, he hurried as fast as he could out the back and away from the estate forever.

CHAPTER 31

After leaving his uncle's, Elliott stayed at Ms. Anna Hakes's guest house for a time, which was separate from the main house but offered enough space and a nice view of the garden.

He had decided when he had saved up enough money to venture away from Gold, he would get a job at a lumber camp so he could travel around and look for Cecilia wherever he went.

"Thanks for cutting the wood today, Elliott," Ms. Hakes called to him as she returned home from her day at the schoolhouse "Winter is coming." She rubbed her gloved palms together. "I can feel it."

"No problem, Ms. Hakes."

"Come in for some supper, when you are done."

"Thank you. I will be done soon."

He came in and sat down with her and another older gentleman that lived upstairs as a tenant in the house named Alfred Whittimier.

When they had all finished eating and Alfred had retired to his room, Anna sat at the table with Elliott.

"There's something I want to tell you."

"What is it, Ms. Hakes?"

"I want to give you the money you need to look for Cecilia."

"What? No, I can't possibly–"

"Please, I want to, Elliott. I know how much you want to find her."

"I can't thank you enough, Ms. Hakes.

Honestly, I will never be able to repay you for your kindness."

"Just go and find her, Elliott. Bring Cecilia Mason back to Gold. Back to her family and to you, where she belongs."

CHAPTER 32

Cecilia and Hawkley made it back to Gold quickly. Hawkley was a talented rider and knew many paths and ways to travel after spending his entire life with the carnival.

"Gold's somehow busier than I last remember," Cecilia said, looking around. "I don't recognize half of these people."

"What's this?" Hawkley pointed to a new sign that read *Main Street.*

"It's a street sign, boy," a rough, gray-bearded stranger who walked like a perched squirrel replied.

"What about that?" Hawkley asked. "What are they building over there?"

"That's fixin' to be a big ol' hotel with great big rooms. Gold's a new town now what with the oil and the Vanguard brothers bein' here and all."

"Maybe I can stay there once it's finished," Hawkley said, turning to Cecilia.

"Don't be absurd, Hawkley! You'll stay with Ruby, Caleb, and I, and that's all there is to it."

"What about your father?"

"I can't hide from him forever. This is my home and I won't be pushed away from it. Our day will come, meeting face to face. For now though, we're going to my friend John's. He'll know what to do."

CHAPTER 33

John sat in his hand-carved rocking chair, the legs creaked against the wooden floorboards as he swayed back and forth. He got up when he saw someone approaching.

"Hello?" He called out. "Who's there?"

"John!" Cecilia replied. "It's me! Sissy!"

"Sissy Mason?" He squinted, trying to make her out. "Is it you?"

"It is, John!" She ran up to the porch and threw her arms around him.

"Who is this you brought with you?"

"This is a friend."

"Name's Hawkley, sir" he said, extending his hand. "Nice to meet you."

"Nice to meet you, Hawkley. Boy, are Ruby and Caleb going to be thrilled to see you, girl. We were all worried about you. I heard what your father tried to do, marrying you off to that downright awful Lyman Steele."

"I know, John. Neither of them would take no for an answer."

"Don't you worry, Sissy, girl. You and your friend can stay as long as you need."

"You really mean it?" She embraced him again. "Thank you, John.

"What about my father? Have you seen him near town lately?"

"I have. He was at the saloon about a week back. I saw him stumble out. Was actually talking to those two brothers. Those two men here for oil.

Quite a bit they've actually been up to lately. Been digging and blowing into the ground with explosives and everything. Sends the hills quaking every morning until evening. They're even building a new hotel in the center of town."

"Those men were talking to Pa? Those brothers?"

He nodded. "Sure enough. I thought it was odd myself. They were walking and talking with him."

"I suspect it's about our land."

"As far as I see it, your pa ain't got much say one way or another what happens to that land."

"What do you mean?"

"I gave it over to you, Sissy. I own it until your sixteenth birthday and then it's yours. I went back to the courthouse a short while back after I heard these men was coming and I had it made so."

"What about you, John? Aren't you afraid they'll come after you?"

"No. I'm not. Not anymore. But, evil does lurk in the hearts of many. Anyways, I'll be headed away in a short while to the west to meet with the traders again. I'll need someone to look after the cabin, like usual."

"Of course."

"Now I think you'd better go and see your sister. She's been mighty worried about you, Caleb too. I just hope your father isn't around."

"Most times he isn't. But these days, nothing seems certain."

CHAPTER 34

It was dark by the time they left John's. He gave them lanterns. Illuminating their faces, they floated through the dark.

"Do you think your pa will be there?"

"I can't say, Hawkley. Maybe."

"What will we do?"

"I don't really have a plan. Just run, I suppose."

"What about your sister? Will she be frightened near-to-death to see a stranger with you?"

"Ruby trusts me. She'll understand when I explain everything."

Hawkley stepped awkwardly over limbs and debris, trying to keep up with Cecilia. They led the horse as well, which got caught every few feet on a cluster of branches.

Ruby was sweeping the porch when they approached. The light coming through the front door shone at her back. The sound of footsteps caused her to stop.

"Hello?" She called out. "Who's out there?"

"It's me, Ruby! It's Sissy!"

Caleb came running through the door, throwing his arms around Cecilia's middle. The force of it nearly brought her to the ground.

"Sissy! Sissy!"

"Whoa! Caleb! It's good to see you," she bent down and scooped him up, swinging him around like they were dancing a waltz.

"Where've you been?"

"Is Papa here?" She looked at Ruby.

"No, Sissy. He's been gone a few days now. Left town for a new lumber camp."

"How have you all been? Holding up well enough with out me all this time I see?"

"That's not true. Ms. Hakes and Elliott have been coming by every so often when Papa isn't here to help with the animals and such."

"And Elliott?"

"He's moved out of his uncle's estate."

"He has?" Cecilia interjected. "Where has he gone?"

"To live with Ms. Hakes."

"Will he be here soon? Is he coming? Do you expect him?"

"No, Sissy." Ruby's head turned down. "He's just left. Gone to look for you."

CHAPTER 35

Cecilia rushed back toward town to Ms. Anna Hakes's house, hoping Ms. Hakes would be able to give her some direction as to where Elliott was headed. But, when she got there, she was surprised to see Elliott walking away from the house with a satchel of belongings packed.

"Elliott!" She called desperately. "Elliott, wait!"

"Sissy?" He couldn't believe his eyes. Dropping his belongings, he ran to her. "Is it really you?" He said, embracing her tightly.

"I missed you so much, Elliott." She inhaled his scent once more; she'd missed it dearly.

"I was just coming to look for you! I've been living and working for Ms. Hakes but was planning to take a job anywhere so I could find you. When you didn't come back, I became so worried. I didn't know whether I should leave and look for you or stay here and wait. Secretly, I knew in my heart you would return one day."

"Everything is alright now, Elliott. There's just one thing left to do."

"What is that?"

"Find my father, and tell him *he's* the one not welcome in Gold anymore."

CHAPTER 36

Elliott went with Cecilia to look for her father in the local saloons. No matter what he was doing or what his purpose was, he made his way through the saloons like a rat through rubbish piles. Hawkley stayed with Ruby and Caleb and promised to keep an eye on things in their absence. He would also be there if he returned.

"Have you seen my Pa?" she asked the dozenth innkeeper they came across, explaining what James looked like. "He has a large scar on his right forearm here," she said, pointing. "From where a tree hit him."

"Sounds like a man staying here now." He replied. "Been here since the day before last. Paid for a week in advance."

"That can't be him."

"Why you say that so assuredly, miss? He had the scar you've described there on his arm. I couldn't mistake it. Forgive me for saying so, but he was so skunk-drunk he couldn't even stand. He was leanin' in front of me in a way that made it quite visible. And, forgive me for also saying so, but it was hard to miss, being such a large and ugly thing."

"But, he never stays this long in saloons and pays in advance—if at all. He usually stays in the camp to save money for drinking."

"Well, nar I say that he didn't pay, miss."

"What do you mean?"

"T'were two men with him. Holding him up and walking him along like that."

"Do you know them? The men he was with?"

"Can't say as I do."

"Were they other loggers?"

"Well, no miss. These looked like businessmen. Clean-shaven with expensive clothes. They looked alike. Like brothers. Except one had black hair and the other yella'."

"That sounds like the Vanguard brothers, Alex and Adam," she told Elliott.

"Sissy, if they don't know your father doesn't own the land, I fear they may have done something desperate."

"What do you mean?"

"They may have harmed him in some way. If a man that owns the land dies without any will or heirs, it wouldn't be hard for them to buy it up."

"We have to find him."

"But, Sissy!" He took hold of her arm as she turned to leave. "Wouldn't it be for the best? For you and all of you, Ruby and Caleb too?"

"What are you saying, Elliott? He might not be the nicest man, but he's my father. I don't have any other. He's all my brother and sister and I have."

He nodded. "I understand. Let's go find him." He turned to the innkeeper. "May we have a key to the room they took out?"

"Sorry, sir. Nae' can do it."

"Why not? This here is his daughter, and she and her siblings are worried for him. Surely, sir," he implored. "You must understand such a situation?"

He thought for a moment. "Oh, alright," he

conceded. "I suppose I could go with uns' to check un' see."

"Thank you, sir. Thank you." Elliott shook his hand emphatically.

"Don't go un' make me regret this now. Come yuns then."

"Yes, sir." He grabbed Sissy's hand, now as anxious as she to find James Mason. Not only did he love Ceclia with all of his heart—he had since the day she had helped him find his way home in the woods—but he also had heard his father and uncle discussing various properties and their crude oil prospects in the past. Now knowing his own kin to be complicit in such business, he could not stand by thinking that his own flesh and blood could be another proverbial hand striking down yet more misfortune upon the Mason family.

The man knocked loudly on the door and no one replied. "Sir!" He yelled. "Some folks is outn' here looking for yuns!" He pounded the edge of his closed fist against the door once more. "Sir! Open up! Thisn's your last chance to open up now, yuns hear me?" He took out a full set of metal keys from his pocket. "Stand back yuns now. Never know what's on the other side of a door."

Elliott and Cecilia took a step back, holding their breath as they waited for the door to open.

At first, there appeared to be nothing. But, then, they took a closer look.

CHAPTER 37

James Mason was dead. His body leaned up against the wall behind the room's haphazard unmade straw mattress. There were no marks or bruises on him, just a pallor over his cold corpse.

"What are we going to do, Elliott?" Cecilia turned to him. "What if they're after Ruby and Caleb next and are already headed to Gold?"

"There is no way to tell, but we better be on our way back to check on them."

They rushed back, not stopping once.

When they reached the house, they were relieved to see Ruby and Caleb outside.

"We found him!" Cecilia called, running to them. "We found Pa!"

"Where is he, Sissy?"

"He's dead!"

The two cried. Although he wasn't a man to be much missed, he was the only parent they had left. Now, they were truly orphaned.

"What happened?"

"We think the Vanguard brothers got to him, Ruby. We think they've been after him since they found out about the oil beneath our land. They don't know Papa doesn't own it."

"He doesn't?"

"No, Ruby. John does until I do, in about two years time."

"What?"

"Pa never owned it. Grandaddy wouldn't agree to sign it over to him, because he was a mean drunk his whole life, and grandaddy knew it. So, he decided to give it over to John, who was more like a son to him anyway."

"So, John's owned it this entire time?"

"That's right. And one day soon, we will."

"What do you think will happen when the Vanguard brothers learn that we own the land?"

"There's no telling, but we better be ready."

CHAPTER 38

Everyone went to John's in the Black Forest. For the time, they felt safer there. They planned to leave Ruby and Caleb there before returning with supplies to the Masons' farm. There they would wait for the Vanguard brothers.

Looking out the window, Caleb saw someone approaching on a spotted gray horse. "Someone's coming!" He yelled. "Someone's coming!"

John peaked out of the corner of the tattered sheet that served as a curtain. "It's Blacksnake! And he's alone!"

"Travelers!" Blacksnake called out as he approached. "I seek your assistance!" He rode quickly, his shirt covered in blood.

John and the others ran outside to meet him.

"Are you hurt?"

"We were attacked by some men. They had large guns with them. Something made contact with my side. I fear it looks worse than it may be."

"Who were they, Blacksnake?" Cecilia rushed to help John get him down from the horse. "Were they fur trappers?"

"No..." he groaned in pain as they moved him. "They weren't those sort. They were dressed differently, like wealthy men or men from another land."

"It must be the oil men!" Cecilia exclaimed. "How far away are they now?"

"A couple miles behind. I led my people a

different way to keep them safe. We had already hidden are valuables, but it would seem they have found out about the riches we wish to protect."

"Are you sure everyone else is safe?"

"Yes. We parted before burying it in the cave. They were gone before those men caught up with us… They won't know where the others have gone. I just hope he has not followed me here. The others separated. If he reaches one of us, he may discover…"

"Try to rest, Blacksnake." They put him in John's bed, and Ruby retrieved a cloth to wipe his head. "Don't worry."

"We have to hurry, John," Cecilia urged him. "They must be getting close to our side of the hill!"

"Sissy, I think it's best you stay here with your brother and sister."

"No, John!"

"You'll be safe here, Sissy. If something happened to you..."

"It won't, John. I swear it. Please, let me fight beside you." He looked into her eyes, pained.

"I suppose. If it's what you wish."

"Thank you, John!"

"John!" Hawkley entered with Elliott at his side. "Where is your ammunition?"

"In the cellar." He looked at Cecilia. "Sissy knows where it is." They exchanged knowing glances.

"Follow me," she told them, motioning forward. "This way."

They gathered all they could and headed back to the Masons', leaving Ruby and Caleb behind hidden beneath the trap door in the cellar.

John showed them where to wait behind the trees. They waited in silence until they heard people approaching on horseback. Cecilia gave the signal to the others that it was indeed the Vanguard brothers and their hired hands. Everyone took aim. Hawkey, eager to help and get the job done, fired first. Unfortunately, he missed. In no time, the air was filled with bullets and lethal projectiles. John began shooting and then Cecilia.

Hawkley stepped out from behind the base of a tall pine and was immediately met with a bullet to his arm. He fell back with a thud onto the forest floor. He scrambled to get back behind the tree for cover.

Cecilia could see who had shot Hawkely. It was Adam Vanguard. Without hesitating, she ran to help him. But, Elliott could see Adam pointing his gun at Cecilia as she ran to Hawkley. As fast as he could, he took up his own gun, stepping out from behind his shelter to aim at the man who had threatened them all.

The shot rang out. At first, nothing happened. Then, Adam Vanguard collapsed, falling off his horse onto the ground. He was not dead but badly wounded, shot in the side.

"Alex!" He called out for his brother, rolling around in pain. "Alex! Help me!"

At that time, everyone stopped firing at one another. Struggling to lift him onto the horse, a few other men came to Alex's aid until Adam Vanguard was positioned on the back of his brother's horse. "Ah!" He griped each time they attempted to move him or he tried to move himself.

"You won't get away with this!" He used all his strength to yell into the woods at his unseen tormentors. "Weak people like you can't defeat me! I'll be back to take what's mine once and for all!" He spit on the ground, grabbing his side in pain as he did so. "Mark my words! *This isn't the end!*"

PROLOGUE

After that day, Elliott moved in with the Mason family and helped out with the farming. It wasn't long after that, Hawkley confessed he had fallen in love with Ruby and started courting her. They ended up married with nine children and exceedingly happy. They bought the house next door to Anna Hakes, which was similar in style and just as beautiful. They did quite well for themselves and visited Cecilia, Elliott, and Caleb often. Caleb stayed with them until he was a full-grown man of 18 years old.

That's when they began working on building a house for Caleb on the other side of the property; a small, modest, one-room log cabin. Although it was similar to the humble home they'd grown up in, it was much nicer, and it was all his. Caleb would eventually marry a nice girl from Gold named Mary Grace.

Alexander and Adam Vanguard would get theirs, and justice would be delivered. But not at the hands of Elliott or Cecilia. It wasn't long after they killed James Mason, that Adam was killed during an explosion at one of the wells, and within that same year, Alex was thrown off his horse, hitting his head and also succumbing to an untimely death.

They never accepted any money for the oil beneath their land. There it stayed, coveted by many but untouched by those who lived above it. Things around the Mason farm steadily remained the same as far as money and those things were concerned. Elliott and Cecilia farmed the land with the help of

Caleb and his wife. Ruby's children would come and visit, breathing new life into the place.

There they would live. And there they would die. John was right, all they had ever really needed was *love, each other, and the land.*

They never used the gold John had given them. They had also never needed to venture out and seek the treasures Blacksnake and his people had hidden from others. It remained in the cave. Protected by rattlesnakes and other natural threats, it was safe from greedy trespassers and thrill seekers–*until one fateful day...*

When Elliott passed away, Cecilia was devastated. She would often pull out a cherished letter he had written to her. Fighting against the painful hours of bitter loneliness, she would look out the window as she remembered as many moments as she could of their life together, waiting for the time when they would reunite once more:

My angel goes with me wherever I go.
When she's not with me, I feel her eyes and I know...

Made in the USA
Monee, IL
22 March 2024